Dear Reader,

I'm a low-maintenance chick. The kind who's happy with the way things turn out and not in need of a lot of extras to sustain me. So, naturally, Destiny thought it would be fun to dump me in Dallas, Texas—Planet Central for appearances and all things material.

Fortunately, I'm also a survivor and found myself a group of great girlfriends—beautiful women who spent massive chunks of their waking hours in manicures, highlights and cosmetic procedures. We got along great, those diamond-loving girls and I. They thought I was a breath of fresh air. Which, translated, meant I needed lots of help. And they were willing to give it. Sadly, it didn't take.

But my experience got me thinking and another low-maintenance chick, Sky Dylan Stone, was born. Dylan's friends think you can tell the depth of love by the weight of the diamond. All Dylan wants is a soul mate, someone to complete her, to set her on fire, capture her spirit, mind and heart. Not an easy find. Until Brad Davis comes along, the long-legged, boot-wearing guy of her dreams. If only he wasn't so busy chasing his own!

Be you a low-maintenance gal or a diamond-girl supreme, we could all use a soul-scorching love. Drop me a line at carlylaine@comcast.net or visit my Web site at http://home.comcast.net/~carlylaine.

Happy reading!

Carly Laine

Sometimes it's okay to be a virgin

Like when you're fifteen or seventeen or hell, even twenty.

I could think of a few other situations when it's not only okay, it's a damn good idea.

Like if you're the heroine of a romance novel and you lost it on page eighty-six to the guy with the big pecs on the cover.

Or you're super-religious and want to wait until you're married.

But lots of times it was *not* okay. Like when life got messy early and things hadn't worked out the way you planned. Your friends were settling down and you hadn't even gotten started yet. Then it was just plain mortifying.

I wasn't sure when things changed, when I quit fighting off the guys who pretended they wanted nothing more out of life than to sleep with me.

All I know is, by the time I was a senior in college, it had gone from being a prize to a problem and I couldn't pay someone to do the deed.

When did sex become such a hassle?

When Size Matters

Carly Laine

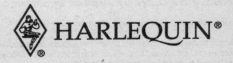

HARLEQUIN®

TORONTO • NEW YORK • LONDON
AMSTERDAM • PARIS • SYDNEY • HAMBURG
STOCKHOLM • ATHENS • TOKYO • MILAN • MADRID
PRAGUE • WARSAW • BUDAPEST • AUCKLAND

ISBN 0-373-44193-2

WHEN SIZE MATTERS

www.eHarlequin.com

Printed in U.S.A.

ABOUT THE AUTHOR

After residing in many places, including Texas and France, Carly Laine currently finds herself living in beautiful Boulder, Colorado, where she spends her days wearing a hard hat and her nights writing about slim-hipped guys with magical smiles. *When Size Matters* is Carly's first novel for Harlequin.

To my family, where the living is easy.

1

DOES SIZE *really* matter? I mean, can how big it is actually tell you anything? Because my friends all think so. They're convinced it shows how much he loves you. As if you can weigh love. That you measure it in carats. Mathematically, it looks like this: carats = love. And, despite appearances to the contrary, my diamond friends excel at math. Increase one side of an equation and they know the other side magically grows with it. More carats, more love. Therefore—and this is the most important part—a really *big* diamond = true love.

The only thing is, I don't know if I buy it.

But if I did, then what I was witnessing on top of the hill that amber afternoon in October was the real thing. Capital *T*, capital *L* True Love. Because the bride's ring was *h-u-g-e*, a diamond doorknob. And as I watched her turn from the makeshift altar they'd set up outside for the ceremony with her new diamond wedding band snuggled against the knob, I thought her left hand hung a little lower and that she had to kind of *drag* it back down the aisle. Think Quasimodo.

I can see my friends if they heard me think that. "D. E.," they'd sing. Knowing for sure that mine was just another sad case of soul-devouring, stomach-cramping Diamond Envy. They could spot it anywhere. And often did. Even if it wasn't. Or maybe it was, I don't know. I do know I wanted some. TL. *Real* love. The kind you could always count on. Lifetime guarantee.

So maybe the real question was this: How do you find *that?* Or rather: How do you *know* you've found it?

I'd been to ten weddings in nine months. That made this one number eleven. Like the Diamond Girls, I, too, am good at math. It was October and—somebody shoot me—there was still another one to go. All things considered, it had been a fairly depressing year.

Number eleven was my fourth bridesmaid gig. The first time, back in April, I was excited. I got over it. My closest friends had trapped me into spending hundreds of dollars on dresses that made me look pale, fat and ugly. Unforgivable what those dresses do to a girl with a chest—think marshmallows, vacuum-packed.

This bride had chosen an anemic rainbow theme for her B-maids, vapid springtime pastels that made us look like little unfound Easter eggs. Faded lumps, lost and forgotten in the autumn leaves. I got stuck with the orange dress—the exact color of that milky, orange, public bathroom soap—because it does really awful things to tawny skin and because, in truth, brides know precisely what they're doing. They know what will make their B-maids look their absolute, unforgettable, all-time worst.

Yeah, yeah, I know, brides say that's not true anymore, that times have changed. But—and I say this with authority based on a great deal of recent experience—there are way too many sorry-looking bridesmaids out there for it to be coincidence.

Number eleven wedding was done up in the high style of the new millennium: overblown and overbudget. Six-figures if it was a dime. They staged it on the groom's parents' spread, a small kingdom chiseled into the Hill Country just outside of Austin, an estate on its own private hill.

When it was featured in *the* architectural magazine—the one that *never* does Texas houses if it can help it—they gushed, and I quote:

> With its creamy blond fascia hewn from the chiseled limestone of the Austin hills, with its patchwork of rooftops quilted in the rusty blues of Texas slate, this magnificent home proudly straddles the hill's rough summit. In the early evening sun, the meandering silhouette forms a miniature golden cityscape, a buttery skyline that peaks and dips in mimicry of the rise and fall of the rock beneath.

Rusty blue? Buttery skyline?

I knew the whole article by heart. It had been recited to me daily, breathlessly, for most of the past twenty-four months. It just so happened that this miniature golden cityscape, this monster mansion with its eye-bugging views of hill and river, lake and sky was more than mere backdrop. It was, in fact, the magic potion, *the* crucial catalyst that had brought the loving couple together. Love at first sight. My friend had seen the place on the cover of the magazine, had fallen in love first with the house and then, after a period of focused Diamond Girl determination, with its only son. Poor guy. Targeted, pursued and bagged before he knew what was chasing him. I guess if you had to marry a house, though, this one wasn't bad. As houses go.

I know that sounds harsh but I was all weddinged out. It had been a long year.

There were two radiant white tents: one for the luncheon buffet and one for the obligatory, inoffensive, soft rock band and parquet dance floor. Each was perched in perfect symmetry on different strata of the hill, as though God had been in a good mood and had designed the terrain for just this oc-casion.

Music, food, a buttery skyline and champagne flowing like the Colorado River below us. It was getting late in the day. There'd been some serious toasting, especially by the father of the groom who was pulling triple duty as expan-sive host, father of the groom and best man. Actually, quad-ruple duty. Add financier to that list. Of the wedding *and* the doorknob diamond. I couldn't look at the guy without thinking, *prime rib*. If you stuck a sweaty face—no neck—and some chunky limbs on those slabs of rare meat oozing under the heat lamps in the luncheon buffet, you'd have yourself a genuine replica of the groom's dad. Should you want one. Which you wouldn't.

He bellowed congratulations to his son, well-wishes for the bride and public introductions of his many, many at-tending business associates. And with each new toast, with each lifted glass, you could hear the subliminal scream, "This is all mine, I did all this. Look at *me*. Look *at* me. *Look at me.*"

Diamonds can be pricey—and I don't mean for the groom or his family. I pictured the carnage of my poor friend's life now, with Mr. Prime Rib in charge. Shudder.

Thank goodness he wasn't *my* problem. Because, orange-soap dress notwithstanding, I was having an amazing time. I'd danced and laughed, and laughed and danced until fi-nally, breathless, I'd had to sneak off to a deserted corner of the dance tent to have a quick gulp of autumn air and ex-pensive champagne. I held myself perfectly still and let the swirl fall away. The light was magic. I even forgot to be cyn-ical for a minute or two. The hill had granted this wedding a special aura, a fairy-tale touch. And as the sun began set-ting, the air took on that perfect glow, that golden glimmer of moments you think you'll always remember.

Oh, what the hell, I said to myself. What if all my best friends were wives and mothers and I was left alone and abandoned, the last singleton in Single Town? *Who cares?* Sure, I was destined to be childless, struggling to eke out a meager joy from other people's kids. *Smile now, smile for Auntie Dylan.* So what? Dancing on top of God's hill, bathed in that silken light, I was content. And as the band launched into a respectable imitation of a salsa beat, I closed my eyes and tilted my head as far back as it would go to let the last, slow drip of champagne bubbles tickle down my throat.

Then I got one of my feelings. One of *those* feelings, where the little hairs on the back of my neck prickle out with the creeps. In my head, I saw one of Spielberg's flesh-eating dinosaurs sneaking up, slobbering, behind me. An arm grabbed me around my waist. The champagne glass banged against my teeth. Hard.

"Dance wi' me," it snarled, its mouth pressed into my hair, reptile lips on the back of my ear, swamp breath on my scalp. I knew that slur, had heard it all afternoon. And as he hoisted me onto the dance floor, I knew that the groom's dad had now become my problem, too.

I am not a tiny girl, not readily hoisted, but I was weightless, fragile in those beefy arms. Centaurs came to mind. Exactly what was it they'd done with maidens they'd snatched?

The thought was pre-empted. With a scowl of fierce concentration, he pressed my arm out to full extension—totally ignoring the crystal flute I still had clutched by its stem—and stuck a dripping jowl to my cheek. We swayed backward to gain momentum and then lunged theatrically forward into a full-body tango. I had to take several quick, ridiculous-looking, little running steps to keep from losing my balance, from being swept, literally, off my feet with my little dyed-to-match orange satin shoes dragging behind me, heels up, across the floor.

"Please don't do this," I managed to gasp when I finally quit trying to swallow my tongue in surprise and actually took a breath.

The band, knowing for sure upon which side their bread was buttered—and by whom—gamely switched to a tango. The dance floor cleared in a flurry of self-preservation. People crowded around the perimeter, unable to spare themselves the discomfort of witnessing my humiliation. And as we raced by their faces, I caught the looks of distaste and nervous glances. Groom Daddy was rich, old and male. Somehow this would all be my fault.

When we reached the far edge of the portable dance floor, I saw the guy I'd come with—finally—rushing to my aid, angling in on us for a cut-in rescue. Sing Hallelujah! I didn't think he had it in him.

But Groom Daddy wasn't having any of *that*. Switching arms without loosening his grip even a notch, he angrily executed that one-eighty tango turn, slammed his pot roast body back into mine and sped with long, bent-kneed strides toward the center of the floor.

"I need to... Please stop," I squeaked out in a pathetic little wheeze. Like a gnat to a rhino, I was ignored.

Okay, okay, think! As my body tried to find some rhythm, some little bit of grace, my mind started whirling with the adrenaline rush. *Options,* I thought, *you have to do something.* Scenarios formed in my head. In one, I'd scream, he'd freeze, the band would shut down. As the echoes of my shrieks vibrated in the silence, the sobbing bride would stumble up the granite steps to the looming stone fortress, dragging her ring hand behind... *Nope, no good.* The bride was my friend, or at least she was before I got stuck with the orange dress. How could I mess up Her Day?

I could swoon and faint, slump against my tormentor in total dead-weight collapse. That might stop him. *Oh, great, Dylan! Then they'd all think you're drunk. You have no choice,* I reasoned with myself. *You have got to pull this off.*

Bracing for further indignities, I composed my face into the amused and tolerant countenance of a good sport. I smoothed the stress from my forehead, brightened my eyes and just as I was working on a sparkly, little laugh, Groom Daddy stopped dead, leaned precariously and flung me backward over his knee in a back-snapping dip. Our arms were stretched overhead, the crystal flute inverted. One perfect drop of champagne splashed on the tip of my nose and slowly seeped inside. All good-sported sentiments drained away as I hung upside down and tears of frustration began trickling up, or rather down, my forehead, the rush of blood and humiliation burning my cheeks.

In another flash, I was restored to vertical and hauled off flailing in a different direction. *Okay, that's it.* Rag-doll helpless was not my style and I...had...had...enough. A cold, clear fury crackled down my still throbbing spine. I hesitated just a moment, debating whether to turn and bite the hair-filled ear attached to the side of my head—*blech!*—or to stick out my dainty orange shoe and trip him violently, midstride. But before I could maneuver my foot into position, Groom Daddy tangoed us—*wham!*—into a guy who'd materialized on the dance floor directly in our flight path.

The impact jostled us around and we bounced off each other a few times until this guy steadied me with a firm grasp on my elbow and eased me off to one side. I shot a quick glance at Groom Daddy and then couldn't look away as he burst into a snarling rage. *Thwarted?* his look said. *You think you can stop me? You. Stop me? N-e-v-e-r.* Apparently you don't get a house on your very own hill by letting things slide.

Oh, God, this was gonna be ugly. I just had the time to wonder, as I slammed my eyes shut, how my high-strung friend—the "everything *has* to be perfect" bride—was going to handle this little digression from the program. I turned away, held my breath and braced for the blast.

And then...nothing.

Risking a quick one-eyed peek, I saw Groom Daddy's scowl had been arrested midsquint and amazement was washing back over his face. The guy bowed to him, low from the waist. And then I, along with everyone else under that tent, watched as he straightened into an elegant long-necked pose, miming a tango embrace with his arms. His voice was low but it rang out in the silence as he politely inquired of Groom Daddy, "Shall we dance?"

No one breathed. But he was *too* perfect—serious, gracious and *so* very ballroom proper. In one giant gust, the crowd exhaled a collective breath of relief and puffs of delighted laughter floated through the saffron dusk.

Even Groom Daddy, sniffing the odds, half chuckled with them. "Aww, let's get a drink," he barked, grabbing the guy's neck with one arm. He raised his other arm to the bartender, hollering for a glass, and dragged the guy with him toward the bar. As he was towed off the floor, taking my place in the prison grip of Groom Daddy's soggy embrace, my rescuer turned to look at me and winked.

Whoa. Just like a movie! I pictured a gorgeous actress lifting her chin, flashing the spectators her dazzling smile and then turning to float imperiously away. I pictured *her*, however, wearing a stunningly simple column of a dress and not the offensive orange pouf. I reapplied my good-sport face, thrust out my vacuum-packed marshmallows and glided off the floor, daintily twirling the delicate and apparently indestructible stem of the crystal flute.

As I cleared the dispersing crowd, my date rushed to my

side. Except he wasn't really a date. Matt was the discarded ex-fiancé of my best friend, Eva. Wounded and hurting, he'd started working on me, trying to convince me that he and I could be more than friends. I didn't buy it. But I did— at the risk of sounding somewhat mercenary—need a date for the wedding. So there we were, not buddies, not dates. Matt took my arm and leaned to whisper in my ear. Solicitous murmurings? Embarrassed apologies?

"Dylan," he said, "you could see everything!"

I cut my eyes at him and gave him my look.

"Your thong!" he groaned and peered anxiously around him to see who was watching us. Everybody.

Thong? My little peach lace thong? A hollow spot began to grow in my stomach. Oh, God! It must have been when I was hanging upside down and my leg flew up in the air. What did a thong look like from that angle? I winced. No wonder everyone was staring. The hollow place turned into a knot. I widened my eyes, trying to blink away the sting of tears. Because I never cried anymore. Ever.

I took a big breath, and... There was the guy, looking right at me, all the way across the dance floor, held captive at the bar, paying too steep a price for his gallantry. A humid hug. Another toast. And Groom Daddy roared, "To the tango, to beautiful girls, to *cham-pagne!*"

I looked at my rescuer. Who was this guy? He seemed fairly standard-issue. Maybe late-twenties or thirty. Hard to tell. Really tall but otherwise pretty ordinary. Definitely not a hunk, but not bad, either. Right then he had hug-rumpled brown hair. *It's too long. Or maybe not... Yeah, no, it's too long. And long legs. Not too long, though, just long. And a dark tan. In October? Probably looks better wearing jeans and a T-shirt than that dark suit.* Then I looked at his eyes, his midnight-black eyes and it was as if he was standing a foot away. I felt a zap, a physical jolt. The skin all over my body shrank up and I could *feel* him, feel the change in the ions between us. I stood there gawking. I just hoped my mouth wasn't hanging open.

Then he grinned.

I forgot all about the upside-down thong, turned and handed my champagne flute to my erstwhile date, gave him a tiny smile and walked straight back into Groom Daddy hell to meet the guy.

2

WHAT WAS IT about an honest-to-God rescue? I swear I would have swooned if I'd been the type. I saw myself—in the movie star's sleek column of a dress—weaving my way across the crowded floor. In my head, no one leered. People smiled and moved aside.

It wasn't just me. We all wanted that perfect someone to waltz—or, even better, tango!—in and deliver us from our dreary, boring, ordinary lives. Someone to save us from ourselves. We've watched *Pretty Woman*, seen the tender young thing being saved by a handsome, rich, charming, intelligent man—in a limo, no less—and we've said, "Right there! That's *exactly* what we want."

I don't think we were brainwashed by the perfect Hollywood story, though. I think we inherited the want from the cave ladies, as with our good eye for color and great gathering skills. I figure the only cave women who survived long enough to produce offspring were the ones who got rescued on a regular basis, it being tricky to run from a saber-tooth while pregnant. We've got a genetically patterned appreciation of the whole rescue business.

If you thought about it, though, it wasn't enough to be rescued. There was that part about the rescuer being handsome, rich, charming and intelligent. We wanted that, too, please. Liberation be damned, we'd like the whole hunky package.

Actually, that's not quite right, not for all of us. Not for the

Diamond Girls. Their definition of happiness had that overriding mathematical bias: perfect someone = rich guy. It seemed the rich part of the fantasy was an adequate substitution for the handsome, charming and intelligent parts. Or maybe more accurately: rich = handsome, charming and intelligent. Automatically.

Not me. I was looking for someone to capture my imagination, to ignite me, to complete me in every way. Mind. Body. Soul. For me perfect guy = soul mate. Tragically, the soul mate had proven to be a lot tougher to find than a diamond.

But now I'd been rescued. In real life. My heart lurched up in my throat and I could feel a silky dampness in my thong. *Dylan! Do* not *think about the thong!*

The guy met me halfway across the dance floor, having taken advantage of the momentary distraction of a passing hors d'oeuvre tray to deliver a good-old-boy whack to Groom Daddy's back, bark a fond farewell and then half sprint away. It had worked. I could see Groom Daddy leaving the bar, storming up the hill toward the luncheon tent, hunting for less agile prey.

The guy walked me through the dancers to an empty corner at the dance floor's edge.

"Thanks doesn't quite cover it," I purred as I tried to arrange myself back into bridesmaid propriety. I made a swipe at my forehead, repositioning wanton curls, brushing sweat salt from my hairline—probably Groom Daddy's... Yuck—and wiping away any mascara tracks running up my forehead. All with—I hoped—one casually elegant stroke.

"Yeah, you looked like you could use a break out there," he said, turning to face me, still grinning out of the corner of his mouth, a mouth just bold-ass *begging* for kisses. "You're Dylan, right? I don't think we've met. I'm Brad. Brad Davis."

I'd like to say that I believed in love at first sight. It kind of went with the whole soul mate thing: when you meet *him*, you will know. I was sure that's the way it would be. But if I'm truthful with myself, I don't think I was thinking right then about love or sight or souls or anything else. I wasn't thinking; I was on fire. Consumed. That was not an every-day occurrence for me. I was usually quite calm. Other girls could go on and on about a guy's this or that—his lips or abs or some damn thing. Blah, blah. I never got it. To me, a mouth was a mouth, like a knee was a knee. I was an eye chick. I didn't have a color preference as long as they were deep, soulful and carried thoughts without words. Eyes spoke to me.

But here was this crooked smile. Lips you could take a nap on, lips that could undo buttons... And then his name wormed its way into my thinking brain. "No!" It was a yelp.

"'Scuse me?" he asked at the damsel's ungrateful re-sponse.

"*The* Brad Davis? Brad Davis of Dallas?"

"Well, not *the* Brad Davis. There's prob'ly more of us up there, if that makes you feel any better. But—" he flicked his hand in the direction of a group of my guy friends standing now at the bar, all sporting goofy smiles as they watched us "—we do seem to have some of the same friends."

Damn. I'd been avoiding this guy forever. There I was thinking about hot lips and they belonged to Brad you-two-would-be-just-perfect-together Davis, the blind date I was never going to have. My guy friends were always trying to set me up with him. Poor old Dylan. And they knew I didn't do blind dates anymore. I'd eventually figured it out that lonesome was loads better than loathsome.

"But," they said, "you'd *love* Brad. Y'all would be *great* to-gether." I knew what they meant by that. *They* loved Brad. All of them. He was a man's guy. All rough and tumble, dirty fingernails from fixing stuff and not very successful. Not the kind of guy who would threaten their egos, but good to hang out with, good to hunt with or bowl with or some damn thing. Perfect for good, old low-maintenance me. It made me mad that they'd think I'd want someone like that. He didn't even live in Austin, but up in Dallas. On top of every other bad thing, he was G.U. Geographically undesirable. Hardly Mr. Perfect.

And here he was, in all his glory. Manly Man himself.

"Oh, um, sorry. I, uh, just wasn't expecting... Well, I mean I'd heard about Brad Davis and thought..." *Get a grip!* I grimaced at him and extended my hand, intending to introduce myself.

Instead, he took my hand in both of his and held it. His hands were strong and hard. Not gravelly like sandpaper, though. Smooth and tough. More like an old shoe. Ooh, romantic. At least his nails were clean. "You're not exactly what I pictured, either. Lemme see. Shapeless clothes, thick glasses. Long stringy hair. Earnest and a little intense."

I pulled my hand back with a jerk. "They said that?"

"Nah." He laughed as he lifted my hand again, pretending to study my palm. "They said I'd love you. A free spirit. Said you'd be *purrrfect* for me."

"So why stringy hair and shapeless clothes?" I asked, but I knew. It was the usual response to my name. I'd been born in '79, aka the reckless years of my mother's life. Her decade of free love, peace and the noble, all-consuming quest for self. She'd named me in one of those classic flashes of seventies free thinking. An innocent act of whimsy and she'd guaranteed—for my entire life—that complete strangers would feel compelled to hunch up their shoulders, squint at me knowingly and exclaim, "Your folks were hippies, right?" I quit answering. The truth was I didn't know. When I was little, I'd once asked my mother if we were hippies.

"Hippies?" she'd giggled, rolling her eyes. "Dylan! Nobody's ever called *themselves* a hippie. They might say, 'I'm into peace' or 'I seek enlightenment.' But—" She stopped and balanced on one leg with her other foot pressed into the knee. She tilted her head to her shoulder, put on a dopey face and raised four fingers in twin peace signs. "Oh, wow," she droned. "I'm a hippie." Then she unwound, laughing her luscious laugh and dropped down so she'd be right at eye-level with me. "Dylan, love, 'hippie' is a word used by people on the *outside*."

I didn't ask again.

Over the years I'd tried out different responses to the hippie question, trying to discover the one that most effectively discouraged further inquiry. I'd abandoned the humiliated silence that I'd used in elementary school when the Jennifers and Ericas first heard my name and sang, "Sky-dle is a hippie. Sky-dle is a hippie." *Outsiders*, I thought. By the time I was in college I was affecting a world-weary shrug and an ironic grin anytime anyone brought it up. But no response had been half as effective as my latest reply, which not only halts the line of questioning, but usually puts an abrupt end to all further conversation. "Oh, no!" I say, fixing them with my best wide-eyed gaze. "We're from New Mexico." The question marks form in a bubble above their heads as I make my escape.

Brad kept his head tilted down, peered at me from under his eyebrows and grinned. He looked quite guilty. And sooo fine.

"It's my name, right?" I asked him.

He didn't say anything. I could tell he wasn't about to get tricked into saying something wrong. He was probably thinking this was a hot spot. Guys are never really sure where the land mines are so they try to be really careful to avoid setting one off accidentally. At least in the beginning, they try.

But I had no hot spots. Not anymore. Just lots of little frozen places. "Don't worry about it. It's my own fake ID, my camouflage. I love my name." And just how dumb did that sound?

"Me, too," he said with not a hint of irony. "Dylan's great."

Now what? I was stuck to the spot. Manly Man appeared to possess some kind of magnet, an intense gravitational pull. I couldn't budge. It always took me a while to get a rhythm going when I was first talking to a guy, even one I wasn't so sure I wanted to be talking to. Or maybe especially then. I just knew I was a whole lot easier with a breezy tempo. I made a stab at it. "I guess I should properly introduce myself. Glad to meet you, Brad Davis. Sky Dylan Stone," I announced, turning my hand into his palm for a shot at a breezy handshake. "Sky with no cute little 'e' on the end."

"Sky Dylan Stone." He rolled it around on his tongue, tasting it and laughing at the same time. I watched his mouth as he said it. All other issues aside, it really was an incredible mouth. It was saying now, "Where'd it come from? Your name."

I took my hand back and looked away from his lips, off to the side. So I could concentrate. "Who knows?" I shrugged. "My mom's been typically vague on that point." I laughed a little then, thinking about it, about her, seeing her again in my head.

"Oh, I don't know, Dylan," she'd said, laughing, when I'd asked about my name. "It seemed like a good idea at the time." Which was her favorite explanation for the stuff she did back then, her only excuse for the reckless years.

I put her away and looked back at him, smiling, plunging

ahead with my breezy tone. "She said the Dylan part came from Bob Dylan. She and my dad really loved that old guy. Still do." And God knows, it could have been worse. She liked Jimmi Hendrix and Janis Joplin a lot, too. Or, heaven forbid, Roy Orbison. I could just hear her. "Well, Orbison, darling, what can I say? It *seemed* like a good idea at the time."

"It's not so bad," I continued, "I like Dylan's songs okay—well, the words to his songs. I think his voice must be an acquired taste." I saw my mom again, thirty-some years ago, in halter top and hip huggers, hair to her waist parted straight down the middle, acquiring a taste for Dylan with a bong and a beanbag chair. "Anyway," I breezed on, "Nobody calls me Sky, except my grandma. Thank goodness. I've been Dylan since birth." I stopped, suddenly aware of the important distinction between breezy and windy, not even sure which parts I'd said aloud. "It suits me just fine," I mumbled, puttering down to a halt.

"Yeah," he agreed. "Kinda no-nonsense and poetic both."

Ooh. I liked that. I stared at his mouth again.

"But Sky..." He let the thought trail. "Sky's magic. Sky...just floats off your tongue."

I shouldn't have been looking at his mouth. I flushed red at the image. It's okay to be a visual person if your visions don't play out on your face for the whole damn world to witness. I pictured myself, legs dangling, head and arms thrown back, floating off his tongue. I blushed.

"So...no more images of shapeless clothes and stringy hair?" I croaked, probably sounding way too earnest and intense.

His look took in the straying curls and vacuum packaging. "No, no. Sorry about that. It's just that I quit trusting my friends ever since they hooked me up with that Dallas Cowboy's cheerleader who was *uncomfortable* with silence. Hell, my ears are *still* throbbin'. But now it's your turn. You tell me. How'd ya have *me* pictured?"

Lord. That smile again. He could have been talking about worm farms for all I cared. I didn't answer. I was thinking that this was what a heart-melting grin must look like. A true Texas-boy smile. Impossible not to get pulled in. That was the magnet. The beautiful teeth, those fantasy lips, the smile that tugged over too far to the right. It made you want to stick around, hang out. *Maybe I could learn to like bowling.*

"Dylan?" he coaxed, eyebrows up.

I forced myself to look up at his eyes, or at least his eye. I could never look at both of someone's eyes at the same time without mine crossing. I just picked one and stared at it. Come to think of it, the saying is "look him in the eye" so maybe everyone does that. I like it when I find evidence that I'm not totally weird.

His eye was pirate black. I could hardly even see the pupil. I looked right at the bridge of his nose to see both of them at once. They were so, so dark, not dazzling like his mouth, but deep and unreadable. I wondered what our children would look like. *Stop it,* I ordered.

His question had hung in the air too long; I decided not to answer. I gazed back at him, smiling my version of Mona Lisa's smile. Then I had this image of a baby smiling when you don't know if it's grinning or having gas and decided to just plain smile. I felt the heat in my body, wanted him to touch me again. The quiet hung between us but it didn't worry me. It was a good thing. Unlike Chatty Cheerleader, Silence would be my friend.

He read the vibes, stepped closer and took my hand again, holding it to his chest, cupped loosely in his. "You wanna go somewhere?" he asked in a kind of croaky whisper. "Now?" If this had been a movie, he would have said,

"Let's get out of here." He was good in this new role, husky voice and all. I knew he knew the effect he had, knew he did it on purpose. He was too close. I wanted to step back, get a little space, but he'd tightened his grip on my hand and I'd have had to yank it to get it loose. I willed myself still and tried to read the vibes, tried to get a sign from those night-black eyes.

And then, pop! The bubble burst. My mom always said I got too tangled up in my own antennae. I felt myself spiraling into rapid cool-down, getting uncomfortable, antsy. I looked around to see if I could see my date, see if maybe he'd like to take another stab at a rescue. He was gone.

I shook my head, telling Brad, no, sorry, no, I was busy. That's what I said to guys who made me nervous. But this time it was true. Somewhere out there I had a date, a date anxious to relive my special moments of humiliation on the dance floor.

"Come on. Just coffee. I'd like to get on out of here. I've enjoyed about all I can stand of the funny looks." He tilted his head at the people walking by, sneaking peeks. I'd been in my own world, thought we were alone. "How about it? We leave now, you'd have time for just a little coffee. Yes?" He stepped back, turned down the heat and cranked up the sunbeam. It looked like it came from inside, way deep down inside.

And I could feel the pull again, tugging. *No way, Dylan. Magnet Man's a player. A rough-edged, hard-handed player. A noncandidate.* I looked away from him, still shaking my head a little, and tried to go through my usual list, those things that I absolutely required in potential candidates. The list I used to talk myself out of guys. Except I couldn't focus. I just knew that he wasn't shorter than me and that he wasn't dumb—that was a guess. It was hard to tell with all those long drawn-out Texas vowels.

I couldn't seem to help it, flopping around from flame to ice to fire again. My friends said I did it so I could stay safe, keep guys from getting too close. But it wasn't that. It was just that I was looking for the right guy. A real guy. Someone I could count on.

It took such a leap of faith.

But here was this guy with the sunshine smile, a guy who made my heart flip and my toes curl. This time I needed to get brave enough to jump. Except my feet were nailed to the floor.

3

BY THE NIGHT of number eleven I'd already had a thousand first dates. Let me make sure that's right. Let's see, a thousand first dates calculates out to about a hundred and eleven first dates every year since my first soul-shriveling date with Cal Richardson when I was fifteen. That would mean at least two first-dates every single weekend for the past nine years... Okay, no, not a thousand, then. But however many there had been, I had a tight, blue rubber band around my heart from each one of those disasters. Pity I couldn't just look inside and count the bands. Like rings on a tree.

Sadly, my second dates numbered somewhat less. Like maybe ten. Steady, long-term relationships had not been my specialty.

If somebody else told me that about themselves, I'd guess the problem was something subtle, not immediately apparent. Like maybe misplaced nipples or braided nose hair. So what was it with me? My super-helpful friends had offered their theories: I was too cautious, I was scared of being left, yada, yada, yada. I had no idea what the problem was, either, but I did wonder why I kept trying. 'Cause it kept getting harder.

Cal Richardson was my first first date. Cal was fairly typical of the guys at my high school—walking hormones with lips. I was so flattered that Cal-oh-my-God-Richardson had asked me out that I floated on air the week before the big date. My feet didn't once touch the ground from the time he called until the disastrous end of the date when I had to put one foot in front of the other as I stumbled to a pay phone to call my mom to come get me. I went out with Cal because he was gorgeous, intelligent and had crystal blue eyes. Cal went out with me to see if my boobs were real. Apparently he and his jock friends were unaware of the phenomenon of girls maturing suddenly and dramatically over the few months of summer vacation. They nicknamed me Mammy, short for mammary. It stuck for a long, long time. And, okay, I'm not going to think about *that* anymore.

The day of number eleven, I'd already had one thousand and one and counting first dates—okay, *really*, some-big-number-less-than-a-thousand plus one with Matt. The guy who wanted to be friendlier than friends. The guy who *didn't* rescue me. A perfect Dylan-style first date. And like so many before it, a date that would have no second date follow-up.

So there I was, searching the reception for Matt, Dr. Nice Guy, trying to think what excuse I'd give for dumping him and running off with Brad the Magnet. Because that's what I was going to do. While I'd been shaking my head "no," feet firmly nailed, I'd started thinking about Brad standing on the dance floor, asking Groom Daddy to dance, heels together, arms extended. My last head shake kind of morphed into a nod, and I heard myself saying, "Yeah, okay, I guess." I tried not to feel that sizzle of fear in my veins after opening myself up like that. I smoothed my face into complacency so he wouldn't think I was flaky, or rather, wouldn't know that I was.

As I looked for Matt, my head kept asking me, *How are you gonna pull this one off? Without lying?* And then he found me.

"Dyl, are you okay? You want to go home?" he asked,

putting his arm around my shoulders as though he was protecting me from physical blows, not just more prurient stares. I saw again what they'd seen, an upside down me, leg waving in the breeze. *Stop thinking about it!* I snuck a peek at Matt. There was no anger evident in him, no sign he was bothered that I'd run off to talk to Brad. Matt and I had been friends a long time. Of course he'd understand. Matt was a practical guy. And careful. If Matt were a girl, his name would be Prudence.

"Yeah, I guess maybe I do." I sounded fairly pitiful. Poor Dylan, ready to go home and lick her wounds. *Liar!*

"You want me to drive you? We could always come back and get your car tomorrow." We each had our own cars because I'd spent the night before at the bride's house, playing lady-in-waiting. Is there just no end to bridesmaid fun?

So there was Prudence, the most serious, dependable guy on earth, caring about me. I hated myself. But apparently not enough to find my way back to the path of righteousness. "No, thanks. I'll be fine." I stared at the grass, avoiding his eyes.

"Are you sure?" he asked, turning to look at my face.

By now I'm thinking, *Yes, already!* "I'm sure. Really."

We went back and forth a few more times. He seemed truly, genuinely concerned. But it came down to this: I couldn't stand not being with Brad more than I could stand being deceitful to Matt. Where was the guarded Dylan I used to know?

Meanwhile, my second first date that day had already been arranged. The Magnet had agreed to meet me at Skinny's after I'd extricated myself from the festivities. We both knew that would take some time. I was in the bridal party, after all.

I was home in twenty minutes. I'd no sooner gotten the words "better go" out of my mouth than the bride had me air-kissed, hugged and sent me on my way to the parking area with an escort. I felt like a fart being fanned out of the room with a towel. I knew the entire Groom Daddy incident would be all my fault!

The phone was ringing as I unlocked the door to my little detached apartment. I kicked off the satin pumps and ran to answer it, guilt propelling me forward, knowing for sure it was Matt, dear Prudence, calling to make sure I was okay. All the way home, I'd been feeling kind of heartsick about the whole thing. I'd messed up again. *Why, Dylan? Why run from such a decent guy as Matt? And to what? A good-ol-boy chick magnet? G.U., financially U., and—if I had to venture a guess—commitment challenged to boot.*

I held on to the wall, did a quick spin around the corner on the hardwood floors, was almost to the phone in the kitchen, when wham! I tripped right over the top of my oversize chocolate Lab bounding around the corner from the other way. Guinness was always late, a burglar alarm on a sixty-second delay. I actually felt myself horizontally airborne a blink before I crashed to the floor.

The orange pouf, with all its unflattering layers of tulle underskirts, saved me, cushioning the blow. "See," I could hear my sunny-side-up mom say as my knees banged into the floor, "Nothing's all bad." Not true. The pouf was bad, all bad.

The phone was still ringing. I'd programmed my answering machine to pick up after nine rings. It helped eliminate all but the most ardent of callers. *How many is that?* I couldn't say; I'd lost count while falling. *Hang on, Matt, I'm coming.* I crawled on stinging knees over to the counter, fighting the dress every tangled-up inch of the way.

guilt = incredible motivator

I reached up to the counter and grabbed the phone. "Hello?" I didn't sound half-bad...considering.

"Hello, little one," my grandma sang out of the earpiece.

I adored my grandma. I can't think of a time when I wouldn't have wanted to talk to her. Except maybe right then. It took me a second to switch gears, to turn off all the what-am-I-going-to-say buzz whizzing around in my head. Maybe it was a good thing, though, that it wasn't Prudence. The whizzing hadn't come up with anything.

"Grandma Frank!" I sang back, trying to sound easy, relaxed. I didn't want to get into it right then, to try to explain my situation to her. First, I had to explain it to me.

"What's the matter?" she asked. I should have known. Grandma Frank could read vibes before they happened.

"Nothing, Grandma. I just tripped over Guinness and I'm really in a hurry. That's all," I said. It was the truth. I had another first date to screw up.

"Speak quickly, then."

"There's nothing. Really. At all. Nothing's the matter." How lame was that? I didn't even believe me.

"And the truth is...?" she asked, patiently.

Grandma Frank was my mom's mom. She lived in a rambling old adobe in Socorro, a dusty little town in the center of New Mexico, famous for its green chile burgers and for having the most powerful radio telescope in the world. Grandma Frank was eighty, lived alone, wove expensive hand-dyed shawls on giant looms, read people's minds and occasionally answered the door to her little hacienda stark naked—spare yourself, don't visualize it. And she was the stable one in my family.

"I don't know, Grandma Frank," I said, sighing, giving up, letting her suck me in. "Maybe you could tell me. Because I can't seem to figure it out."

"You have a date tonight." She didn't ask it like a question. She already knew. "That's good? You're pleased?"

"Well, it's not really a date. A date is something you plan. In advance. This is more like a—"

"Sky, darling," she interrupted. I loved it that she called me that. It meant I was someone else in Grandma-world. "Maybe you're too rational," she said, chuckling to herself. "It's important also to listen to your heart."

"Yeah? What? And end up like my mom?" I asked her, sounding a little harder than I'd intended.

"But your mother's very happy."

"Yeah." I tried laughing but it came out like a snort. Note to self: *You might want to work on that ironic laugh.* "She makes damn sure of that. Nothing else matters. If happiness was a church, she'd be kneeling at the altar."

It sounded so harsh in my head when I did the instant replay. *Wow, Dylan,* I thought. *Where'd that come from?*

"From deep inside," my grandma said. "Sometimes it's good to hear what you think. Helps you decide if it's true. Happiness is good, too, Sky." She continued speaking, not waiting for my comment. Or maybe not wanting to risk another snort. "What is it going to take to make you happy?"

"I don't know," I said. But I did. *Someone who would always be there. With or without the diamonds.*

"Ah, yes, if only it were that easy," she whispered. "You go now. You're in a hurry. I love you." Then she was gone.

The wood floor was hurting my knees. I settled onto my butt. The bridesmaid dress puffed up in front like a just-landed parachute. Guinness came and sat on his haunches beside me. Maybe I wouldn't go, instead just stay here with Guinness, in my hideout, where things were uncomplicated and I was safe. I put my head against his. "No offense, Guinness, but I like it that you're so simple." He jerked away. Offense apparently taken.

I took his big head in my hands and looked him right in

the eye. "So, my little pet," I told him nose-to-wet-nose. "What's it going to take to make *you* happy?"

Guinness stuck out his tongue and gave me an enormous Lab-kiss. And then couldn't stop because, *slurp-slurp-slurp,* Groom Daddy sweat was too yummy to resist.

4

I'D BEEN LATE getting to Skinny's. With all that time to spare I'd still managed not to make it on time. No wonder we drove guys crazy! I'd felt better after my talk with Guinness, had taken a quick shower and raced around my apartment trying on different outfits. Good thing my roommate, Andie, hadn't made it home from the wedding yet, to delay me even more, asking a billion questions I couldn't answer. I did have to keep stopping to explain to Guinness that we weren't playing fetch. But that wasn't why I was late. I'd felt so relaxed in my jeans, short sweater and favorite tennies—really, for the first time in ages—that I'd decided to walk down the long hill from my apartment to the coffee shop instead of driving. Or maybe I was stalling. I never know with me.

Brad was still wearing his suit pants and dress shirt, but he'd pulled off his tie, undone the strangle button on his shirt and rolled up the sleeves a couple of turns. One yummy look.

He was waiting for me in the parking lot, leaning against his old, faded-blue BMW and looking out over Lake Austin, that lengthy stretch of the Colorado River where they've dammed it up on the West side of town. I could feel the lick of the flames again as I walked up to those long, long legs. Brad pushed himself off the car—no hands, just legs—told me I looked great and kissed my cheek. There were those lips again, wrapped around the off-center smile. Matt who?

Skinny's was a big deal to me, my wild life refuge, a place I went by myself not to be lonely. And I never shared it with people who wouldn't be good to run into at a ragged three in the morning or at ten o'clock on a dateless Saturday night. Brad lived in Dallas, which made him pretty safe.

"Hey, thanks again for the rescue," I said to fill the silence while we were waiting in line, perusing the pastry case. "I'd been about to do something dire." It came out breathless. Maybe because of the gravitational pull.

"My pleasure," Mr. Magnet replied. I could hear the smile in his voice. "I'm not really all that fond of bullies."

"Yeah, me neither," I answered, witty conversationalist that I am, apparently out of brains as well as breath.

And that was the end of that conversation volley. The quiet grew so thick, it was like having another person there. Then I remembered what Brad had said about Chatty Cheerleader and my vow that Silence was my new best friend. She inched forward in line beside us.

I looked back over my shoulder at him. He stepped closer and smiled. I started rationalizing—we excel at that in my family. Really, Dallas and Austin weren't all that far apart, less than an hour away on Southwest Airlines. By car, they were hooked together with a straight, flat, slice of the same freeway that linked Mexico to Canada. You just got in the left-hand lane of I-35, set the cruise control for 84 miles per hour, leaned back and prayed. And there was a lot of interface between the people in the two cities. That's what Brad and I could do, interface.

We moved ahead one half step. Skinny's was quintessential Austin. Besides the best coffee, Skinny's could claim the most sinfully decadent desserts on earth. The owner had the genius idea of hiring *two* pastry chefs: one French pâtissier and one local Austin guy, each to create their own desserts. Hot-blooded sparring between the two had given birth to such creations as Mocha-Morning Blossoms and The Czar's Chocolate Clouds, Aphrodite's Cream Puffs and, my favorite, Cupid's Toes in Cocoa Sauce. Skinny's wasn't very big and sometimes the cozy little rooms with the overstuffed chairs weren't enough to hold the multitudes that crowded there after movies and night classes and on weekends. It didn't matter. There was always space. Outside, on both sides of the little shop, were acres—okay, maybe not *acres*— of wood decking, at different levels. On mild nights, like that night in October, you could take your Cupid's Toes, find a private little world at a table under a gas lamp and contemplate life, talk or just sit there and watch the boats putter by on the lake.

We waited until we'd finally gotten our coffees and cakes, found a secluded table outside and sat down across from each other before we said anything more. "Sorry I let it go on so long. It took me a while to come up with a plan," he chuckled. I could see him remembering. I hoped he'd had the face view.

"Well, it was perfect and I thank you." It had come out like a coo. As though I was saying, "Oh, you're so big and strong...and poor little me." Except I'm not a very good cooer; I run out of pucker too fast. "You were there on the groom's side?"

"Yeah, roommates at U.T. Used to play squash, have a beer together whenever I was in town. Good guy. Or he was," he said wistfully.

"Married, remember?" I reminded him. "Not deceased."

"Well, I haven't seen him once since she got her princess-cut boulder. Think she'll let him out now?"

Good point. End of another conversation volley. Dylan: 0.

It was Brad's serve. Silence sat down, hung around, watched the boats with us. And then finally, he said, "So, what do you do?"

"I'm a bridesmaid. Certified."

He smiled his smile. Thank goodness. When you joke around as much as I do, you have a better-than-even chance of a flop. "Full-time?" he asked, eyebrows up.

"Nope. Believe it or not, it's actually not much of a moneymaker. I have to sell stuff to support the habit." I realized, all of a sudden, that I hate telling guys what I do. It was one of those midchat epiphanies I get sometimes. And midchat, I started to wonder why.

"Like what stuff?"

"Services." It wasn't the job I hated, so much. I was new at it but that wasn't it. The real problem was trying to explain my industry to people who had no idea what the whole thing was about. It could get painful. They usually ended up saying something like, "Yeah, okay, whatever."

"Are you makin' me guess or somethin'? All right...I know. Wedding services? No, no. I got it. Dance lessons."

At least he didn't say peep show. "Professional." Now comes the painful part.

"What kind?" he asked.

"Um...professional services."

"Yes, Dylan, I got that part," he laughed. "What...*kind* of...professional...services?" His slow Texas syllables got even slower. As though I was deaf. Or *really* stupid.

I didn't want to get into all this. I wanted us to be on the same page. I can't believe I said that. I *hate* that stupid expression. But I knew Manly Man wasn't going to know about all this stuff and it was going to get embarrassing. For both of us. "How do you like Cupid's Toes?" I asked.

One eyebrow shot up. I'd kill to be able to do that. *Maybe I should start interpreting his eyebrows instead of his eyes.*

"Your little cakes," I answered the eyebrow.

"Dylan," he said with a big, exasperated sigh. "This is real painful. Are you gonna tell me what you do or not?"

"I sell professional services. B-to-B. Um, that's business-to-business—Internet logistics, human contact technologies. Stuff like collaborative browsing." I waited for the zone-out.

"What? Like e-Boost?"

Okay, maybe someone else could have seen that coming. If I'd had any fillings, he'd have had a great view. It took me a while to get my jaw back in its socket. "That's my company," I said with a big, old, toothy grin. In the collaborative browsing world, happiness *is* being on the same page.

"Sales, huh? Seems like I'm remembering somebody told me you were a programmer or analyst. Designer or something like that. Something super...nerdy." He gave me one of his scrumptious grins so I wouldn't be offended. I pursed my lips and pretended to consider it. But I was really just thinking about his mouth.

And then I got the uneasy feeling that maybe he knew more about me than I knew about him. Like maybe that's where he'd gotten the idea about thick glasses and stringy hair. Another midchat epiphany: *Duh, Dylan. It's the job, not the name.* Damn. I'd rattled on about my name for no reason. Talk about paranoid. *Get over the name thing, Dylan. Lots of people have weird names—Pawnee, Breeze Zed, not to mention Keanu and... Rats! What had my friends said about him?* I couldn't recall. Did he really bowl and skin opossums and pick his teeth with a knife? No clue.

He was waiting with Silence.

"Yeah, I was. All of the above. Except for the part about being nerdy." I gave him a little stink eye for that. "In the business, we prefer to call it technical," I informed him. He kept grinning at me, enjoying himself. "But I decided to get into sales instead. Something opened up and I went for it."

"Why?" he asked.

I had to think a little about what to say in response. There was no way I was going to tell him the real reason.

"Money?" he guessed, while I was doing my pondering.

"No, not really." I mumbled it.

"Did you like your job, like being...technical?" he asked.

"Yeah. I did. It's who I am."

"Then why?" He really wanted to know. This was one of those first-date tests, I could tell. What if I did switch for the money, was he going to think less of me? Probably. And why did I care what he thought? Because I did. For some dumb reason, I cared a lot. *And why do you suppose that is, Dylan?* I asked myself. *Because,* I answered a bit testily, *gravity is one hell of a force to resist, that's why.*

"If I tell you, could we talk about you for a while?"

"Sure, if you want. Not much to tell."

"Deal," I said. "But you're going to be sorry you asked, and, okay, here it is. I got out of development because I have a good friend, Rex, who's one of the best technical guys I've ever seen and we were talking one day and he said if I wanted to be really good at it—I mean, really, really good— then I'd have to turn off certain areas of my brain so that more blood could flow to other parts, the analytical ones."

His left eyebrow rose slowly toward his hairline.

I ignored it, took a breath and pushed on. "And the parts Rex was talking about shutting off were the social parts, the parts that care about other things besides geeky stuff, the parts that make normal people different from techies. I thought a lot about what Rex had said and I knew what he meant. And also knew he was right. But I couldn't do it, didn't want to do it—I like those social parts—so I got out."

Both eyebrows were up. He just sat there looking pleased.

It was essentially the truth. My decision had been only a little bit about the money. Okay, maybe more than a little bit. But did I pass his test? I wanted to pass. I could tell he was getting ready to follow up with a whole barrage of other questions. I'd never been with a guy who wanted to talk about me so much. You think that's what you want, what'll make you really happy, but then it happens and it's sort of weird. I cut him off before he could launch them. "Okay. It's your turn. How did you know about e-Boost?"

I could see him switching gears. Whatever he was going to say about my career strategy, he let it go. "A while back I was considering contracting with them. But—" he took a breath and tried to make his voice small "—*Y'all are tooo 'spensive,'* as my little sister would say."

What a tempting serving of data that was, all piled up and steaming on the output platter. It looked as if Silence was going to be gone for a while. Which tidbit to munch on first, family or job? I'm a sucker for kids. "You have a little sister, too? How old?"

"Four. She's my half sister. Emily. She's my dad's kid with his new wife. But, man, she's a great little kid." His grin got even bigger, if that's possible. Or maybe it got less lopsided.

More data. My mom always said to avoid relationships with men from broken homes. This from a woman who'd busted up at least three.

"We're not allowed to say that," I told him.

"Which?" he asked.

"Half. I have a half sister, too, but my mom turns purple if anyone says that. 'There are *no* half people in *my* house.'" I did a pretty good impersonation of her.

"Hey, I agree with that. Emily's my sister. She calls me bro. So you got any others? Halves or steps or…half steps?"

I thought we were going to talk about him. How did we get down in this Dumpster so quick? It was one of the few situations where I followed my mom's advice. "Avoid revealing the details," she always said, "until they're hopelessly in love and less likely to bolt."

But it was getting embarrassing avoiding his questions. I

opted for a quick, emotionless inventory. Be honest, be light, get it over with. "Yeah, I've got a few. Let's see—one current stepfather, one current stepmother, four ex-stepmothers who each had a kid, so three ex-stepsisters and one ex-stepbrother, three ex-stepfathers, so add one more ex-stepbrother, one half sister—no make that one real sister who had a different dad—and one real brother who has a *really* different dad. Is that right? No, sorry. Only three stepfathers, total. She didn't marry Asia's dad."

I'd caught him midbite. He didn't react or say anything, just sat there slowly chewing the little cocoa-dipped toes, watching me. His eyes scanned mine, then my mouth, my forehead, down again to my mouth. He swallowed, took a sip of coffee, swallowed that, eyes studying me the whole time.

What? That was supposed to be light. What would he have done if I'd gone into some of the nauseating details? Bolt?

I'd sure been wrong about one thing: Silence was back, filling the space. Boats floated by, people at the other tables talked and laughed and no one at this table made a sound.

Then a picture of Dr. Matt Sears, erstwhile wedding date, popped into my head. I saw him like one of those white mannequins in the window of some posh store, wearing nice shoes.

"Hi," a voice said before he appeared. "I thought I'd find you here." And his Cole Haan loafers stepped into our silent little world under the gas lamp.

"Hey, Matt," I said, looking up at him and smiling, and willed myself physically out of the equation. Whatever happened next, I wasn't going to be one of the parameters.

Matt put out his you-could-have-been-a-surgeon hand and said, "Hi. Matt Sears. And you must be the White Knight."

Brad beamed his smile in Matt's direction, stood and introduced himself. We were all just *so* happy to be there.

I was left looking at trouser flies. We don't like to do that nearly as much as guys think. Eyes, I liked gazing at eyes. I moved over on my bench to make room for Prudence. "All right," I said. "Everybody sit. I'm getting a crick in my neck."

Brad said, "Yes, ma'am," and sat.

Matt watched Brad sit and then looked back at me, amused. "No, thanks, Dyl. I was just dropping this by your house. Your Jeep was there and you weren't so I figured you'd be here." He handed me a white napkin. "I'll see you guys later. Nice meeting you, Brad." Prudence was always nice. Super nice.

Brad raised that eyebrow of his. "Dill? Like pickle?"

I shrugged, thinking about the napkin and what was inside.

We stared at each other a minute and then I unwrapped it. A champagne glass. I set it on the table between us.

"Oh," I said. That was a loaded "oh," meaning, "What in hell?"

"A souvenir," Brad answered.

"Oh." This time I meant "Souvenir of what? Me leaving with another guy?"

"Or," Brad suggested, "it was an excuse to come see you tonight."

No comment. I was visualizing Matt walking back to his car alone, head down, shoulders slumped. One of those sad country songs playing in the background. This was Austin, so the singer would be Willie Nelson. I didn't exactly know any of the words to his songs, but probably he'd be singing something about hell is having a heart in this heartless old world.

"Who *is* Matt?"

"A friend."

He looked at my eyes a minute. One at a time, back and forth. "And who is Asia?"

I laughed. Because it was good to not be talking about Prudence. I'd been holding the guilt off, but just barely, and my wrists were getting tired. "Asia is my sister. My beautiful, mysterious, little sister. Asia Cézanne McKay."

"Man, I love these names. What's your little brother's name?" Jeez, he'd heard that part, too.

"Greyson. Greyson Carter McKay. We call him Grey."

His lips worked their way over to the right into his sexy, crooked grin. The one that showed all of his pretty white teeth. I may have mentioned it....

"Their last names are both McKay? I thought you said they had different dads."

"Yeah, that's right, but remember? We were talking about you and *your* family."

"We were?"

We weren't but I nodded my head.

"I got a mom who didn't remarry, a dad who did, a stepmother a couple years younger than me and a real sister, Emily."

I tried to keep my face impassive, the whole time thinking, *Whoa! Younger than you?* Out loud I asked, "What's that like?" Seemed like the Magnet Man and I had some family tree mutations in common.

"Oh, you know, strange at first. But she's a good mom to Emily and a nice tasty treat for the old man. She and I get along okay. Not *too* friendly, though." He chuckled to himself, popping his eyebrows up and down. "She's pretty hot."

Trophy wife. Arm candy. I named her Candy Love. Man, oh, man. You just knew Candy Love was a card-carrying Diamond Girl.

"Big diamond?" I asked.

"Huge," he answered, deadpan.

I knew it! Older = bigger. At least when it came to men and diamonds.

We sat at our little table, pleased with ourselves, as though we shared some secret or maybe an inside joke. I didn't need my grandma's antennae to read the vibes. He wasn't into the whole carat thing. You could just tell. And I was grinning, letting him think we were on the same page. But I wasn't really *opposed* to carats. In fact, getting some would be nice, before I was too old and wrinkly to wear them. I knew they didn't measure love. But if love went with it, a little, itty-bitty carat—or three or five—would have been fine with me. I got squirmy then, knowing I was deceiving him by allowing him to think I was above it all. And then the air changed, the moment was gone.

Acting on some parallel cosmic impulse, we both reached for the champagne glass at the exact same time and knocked it on its side. It didn't break. Of course not. If it could withstand Groom Daddy's affections it could withstand anything. Brad reached for my hand with one of his and used his other one to hand me the glass. I took it but he didn't let go and we became a completed electrical circuit. Switched on.

"You gonna keep it?" he asked, lightly rubbing my palm with his thumb, increasing the voltage.

I barely nodded.

"Good," he whispered.

Another nod from me. What that thumb was doing to my insides!

"And, Dylan," he said in that soft, growly voice of his. "I wanna promise you something…"

This time, I just let my eyebrows speak. Up they went.

Both of them. I sat very still, watching him across the table and holding my breath. Waiting with Silence.

"Sky Dylan Stone, I promise I, Bradley Hamilton Davis—"

Oh, nice name. But I wasn't about to distract him.

"Also known as *the* Brad Davis and Brad Davis of Dallas—"

No breath would pass my lips until he finished.

"—will never, ever—" he said, dropping his voice even more, but still managing to heat up the "ever." He paused and looked right into my eyes. Both of them. At the same time. And his thumb kept circling my palm. "—ever...call you Dill."

I took a deep breath and looked past his upturned lips, straight into the quiet of his charcoal eyes and I felt the rubber bands around my heart begin to snap apart, one by one, and that big, hard knot inside of me start to melt away. And I fell again, for the second time that day. Crashed hard. But this time there was no puffy orange dress to break my fall.

5

WE LEFT Skinny's in the middle of a raging electrical storm. It wasn't the drenching kind that we usually had in Austin, with water flooding the curbs and broken tree branches dragging down the power lines. This was more like a New Mexico storm where the sky spits fire—all dry crackle and flash—and zaps until the air gets that weird, edgy feel, like impatience or maybe anticipation. That balmy, October night in Austin, it wasn't the whole sky that flickered with fire, only the part in between us. And that part was smoking.

We worked our way up the levels of decking, past benches and tables, hand in hand, generating our own private atmosphere, making the molecules dance. It wasn't just me; I knew that. You can't cook up that kind of turbulence without two weather machines. We were moving slowly, savoring the suspense, and had just come upon a table in the front close to the sidewalk when I heard Matt's voice, low and laughing. I'd know it anywhere. Matt laughs like he's saving his energy for something else. So much for slumped shoulders and sad country songs. He was sitting with a group of people I didn't know, mostly guys, probably some of his doctor friends. He saw me notice him and raised his glass, a no-expression expression on his face. Everyone at the table turned to look. Brad and I waved back with our unheld hands and we sizzled by without stopping. How lovely it would be, I thought, not to run into Matt anymore.

We reached Brad's car in Skinny's parking lot, looked at each other, smiled, and got in without saying a word, neither of us mentioning that I'd told him at the wedding that I was busy, that I had plans for the night. Silence rode in the back and stayed with us the whole two and a half seconds it took to get up the hill and around the three bends to my apartment. Okay, it took about five minutes but he was flying. I think he actually straight-lined the drive and avoided the curves altogether. Maybe not, I was afraid to look.

He parked to the side of the big house—where you have the best view of the lake—and before the engine had *kachunked* to a stop, his hardened hands were holding my face as if I was the most precious thing in the world and he was kissing me. And if I'd died right then at least I'd been kissed. Really kissed. Those beautiful lips came down on mine and he drank me in, as if I was water in the desert, as if he'd never drank before. His lips were so soft—but not too soft—and his tongue was pressing without being scary. His hot mouth became my world. The power of it sucked me in and sent me tumbling in the dark.

He ended that kiss with another one that was even better followed by three small kisses, little sucking pulls on my lower lip. Then his lips were gone and I just felt his strong hands on the sides of my face. I didn't move. He leaned over and again brushed my lips with his and finally, I opened my eyes.

He fell back into his seat and looked out the windshield at the lake. There was a soft breeze messing up his hair a little. That was one of the best things about being by the water— the gentle winds. Breezes kept our little corner of Austin from having that help-me-Jesus-I-can't-breathe sauna-feel you get in the other parts of the city. I could see the heave of his chest, as though he'd just run up the hill instead of flying. I put my hand there to feel the rise and fall and he covered it with his, closed his eyes and smiled.

The crunch of tires on gravel chased away Silence as Andie pulled up in her little red Miata. If she saw us sitting there in Brad's car, she gave no sign. I watched her jump out of the car, gathering the pale blue bridesmaid dress into a bulge as she ran inside. She looked great. It'd take more than a horrid dress to do Andie in. Many seconds later, Guinness barked his belated greeting at her.

"My roommate's home," I said.

"So I hear." His head was tilted back, eyes still closed.

"Maybe we should stay out here," I suggested.

"Whatever," he said.

Uh-oh. Was he already losing interest?

I got out of the car, cooling off the exact number of degrees that he had. Or trying my damnedest to do so. I leaned against the hood of the car, and wondered what the hell I'd been thinking. The guy I've been waiting for my whole life hadn't been waiting for me.

After a little while, or maybe a long while, Brad got out and leaned on the car next to me. He put his arm around my shoulder and pulled me in to him, pressing his leg into mine.

Hot, cold, hot, cold. What was the deal here? I felt as if I was dangling in space, hanging out over the water. I turned my head slightly away, tried to get my feet nailed back down on firm ground. I spoke but I couldn't get the real question out, the one I wanted to ask. So I settled for a lame "You're in construction, right?"

He didn't answer, just kept his arm around me, rubbing my back. He could have swept me up and swallowed me whole if he'd wanted to. Instead, he barely kissed my ear, my neck and then said into the crook of it, "Yeah, I have my own company. Commercial construction."

The part of my brain that was still working thought about that. Construction. Hard work. Hence the tan, the hands, those strong arms inside the rolled up sleeves. The long, tight legs.

He pulled away again, let his arm fall down on my waist.

Okay. I get it. We're playing the old game of Restraint. The most nonchalant one wins. I was good at this, had been playing all my life. I cranked myself in and croaked out, "Why'd you need e-Boost?"

He pulled away some more. "We put our project plans on the 'Net," he said, all business now. If I wasn't careful, he was gonna win this game. "Time lines, permits—they all go up."

But I was world-class at Restraint. Or at least at being repressed. I pulled back, too. So now only our hands were touching. My breathing was back to normal. Almost.

"Who'd you use instead of e-Boost?" I asked. *If they had sent me up to Dallas, I would have sold him.* Winning Restraint game strategy: Think about work not about his hands, strong and smooth, holding mine.

"Just us. I used to work for a couple of start-ups," he said. Mr. Easy Cool. *Man, he's good.*

And then I thought, *This is all right. Talking like this. Getting to know each other. It's nice. It's good.* I just wished he would kiss me again. His hands on my face. His mouth...

"So, I still had some contacts from that, around the metroplex," he went on. His voice was becoming animated—*about work!* No restraint now. "I put together a team. Formed a new company. Man, we had a rough time, starting out. Worked every night and all weekends 'cause my partners had day jobs and I had real buildings to put up. We got it figured out, though. The slickest way to do the pages. And we started offering the service to the big guys, contractors and subs, first in Dallas and Fort Worth, and then all over the state."

"Are you technical?" I asked. I knew he wasn't. I could always sniff out the techie guys. Sometimes literally. But I needed to show him how casual I was. Casual and brain dead.

"Are you asking if *I'm* a geek?" He smiled, teeth glowing in the moonlight. "Naw. I understand it all on some level, but I'm mostly the idea guy. My partners have to do the dirty work. They like it though. I think a couple of them have those brain lobes you were talking about. The ones that are permanently shut off."

I liked how he'd heard what I said, even when I was babbling. And I *really* liked the way his voice sounded in the dark—soft and rumbley. Maybe this was turning out okay. The electric storm had simmered down to a kind of background turbulence. We looked at each other, glanced out over the water, then looked back. It wasn't fireworks and shivers now. It was...what? And then one of my mom's words popped up. *Mellow.*

"What services do you offer?" I asked, letting myself get into it, learning about him.

"You name it. We're just getting started. Six whole customers. But they're big. The coordination they need on a job can be staggering. So they contract with us to solve that." As he talked, he forgot to sound as though he'd only made it through a third-grade panhandle education. He still stretched out some of the words and cut other ones short—but that's like any good Texan.

"The 'Net gives you a control center." He kept holding on to my hand and, as he explained, he'd lift and motion with it as if it was his own. Up our two hands would go, two beats for emphasis, then down again. He seemed happy to have someone to talk to. Someone outside of work who could understand what the hell he was talking about.

"Our stuff isn't flashy—it's workhorse, B-to-B comm. We give 'em fast, easy, intuitive access to all the critical information. Did I say intuitive? Make that bombproof. The users are construction guys, not your average computer wonk." He took a breath and cocked a smile at me. "No offense." Then he got right back into his pitch. "It's all about coordination. Coordination, collaboration and control."

Our clasped hands beat the air three times. "Coordination, collaboration and control, oh my!" he chanted.

"Oh, my!" I echoed, lifting our hands up together and dropping them again in my lap.

He grinned. "Sorry about that." He let go of my hand. *No!* "We're pushing so hard right now. It seems like that's all I do. Plug our stuff. I can't seem to talk about anything else."

How about we talk about us! "I know," I said, serene as could be, as though I didn't want to reach up and touch his hair, and curl into those sturdy arms. "It's the curse of sales. Everything's a pitch. Man, but you should hear my roommate, Andie. She sells on a turntable…" I stopped. I saw Andie in my head, with her incredible red hair and those freckles on her satin-brown skin. I turned toward our apartment and waited.

"Turntable?" he asked.

I put up a wait-a-minute finger.

"What is it? Dylan?" he asked after a couple of beats.

"Andie's coming out," I whispered. And one long minute later, counted out by a few breezy sighs from Silence, we saw Andie and Guinness appear in the door and step into the night.

"Guinness," I called. "Here, boy."

Brad looked at me, looked at the dark missile streaking toward us and braced for the impact.

But Guinness is a classy dog. He's been trained. He knows not to be ordinary and obnoxious and jump up on people. He shot over to my side of the car, threw his front paws in my lap and did a little half hop up so he could give me a huge, wet, chin kiss. Sometimes Guinness forgets, but he's still classy.

"Down," I said, wiping my chin with my sweater sleeve. He obeyed. I pointed my finger at him. He sat.

"I thought that was you when I drove up," Andie said when she reached the car. "I'm sorry I didn't stop. But I was going to get real ugly if I didn't get out of that damn dress." She looked at Brad and showed him her dimple. "Hi, I'm Andie."

His hands were free. Unfortunately. He reached for her tiny hand and engulfed it. "Brad."

"Don't I know," she said, rolling her eyes at me. "No one's been talking about anything else. Nice rescue."

I watched Brad to see how'd he'd react. Andie was a petite porcelain doll from the piney woods down in East Texas. Except don't think Hummel figurine. Andie was black porcelain with incongruous red hair and freckles. That hair had caused Andie no end of hurt when she was growing up. Her father never did believe she was his. There was something breakable about Andie—probably from that beat-down childhood in those piney woods—and it made guys get all mushy inside, made them want to scoop her up and take her home to mama. Especially big guys.

But there was no sign of scooping from Brad.

"Where you going?" I asked her. She was all dressed up for going out. Red, red and more red—to match her hair—with a few shots of gold. All of it tight and short, except the shoes. They were high and strappy.

"What did you do to your hair?" she asked reaching over and ploinking one of the curls by the side of my face. It brushed my cheek as it snapped back up. "This isn't Dallas, honey. 'Member? We don't do big hair down here. We have class." She flipped her eyes over to Brad, to let him know she was teasing about Dallas, even though she wasn't. He just showed her his lopsided grin.

I stuck the curl behind an ear. I always forgot to primp. I could just imagine my wild-woman-of-the-forest look culminated from the walk, from the electric storm, from the flight up the hill, from those kisses. *Those kisses.* I replayed them in my head and could actually feel the heat of his mouth again. I reached back to gather my hair. Brad stopped my hand.

"No leave it. Please," he said. "It's great."

We smiled at each other as I let it back down. Wow! A Texas guy who didn't think I had to be Barbie groomed all the time. Actually, I *had* that look. Just not brand-new out-of-the-box. More like after the doll has been tossed naked into the back of the closet for a couple of months—wild-eyed and woolly.

Andie stood off to the side, watching us. Several seconds must have ticked past as Brad and I communed with our vibes. Nobody can watch that for very long.

"I'm going down to Sixth Street," she broke in, holding up her cell phone. "They're gonna call me and tell me where. Y'all wanna come?"

I didn't look at Brad. I wasn't ready to share him. "Nah. It's Sunday night..." I said, sounding ridiculous. Sunday night was hopping in Austin.

She didn't say anything, just looked at me expectantly, as though I could read her mind and... *Oh. She must be going out with Prudence and company.*

"Sure?" she asked when she saw me get it.

"Yes," I said. "Go. Have fun!" I called to her as she

walked away. "Don't wake me up when you come in. *I* have a job."

"I have a job," she tossed back. "It's just a good one."

"Did you want to go?" I asked Brad after Andie was safely in her car, peeling out of the driveway.

"Did I get a vote?" he said.

"Well, she was going with Matt and his friends..."

"Oh." He digested that for a minute. "How do you know?"

"I could just tell."

He watched my eyes in the dark for a minute. Guinness had unseated himself and was nosing around. Brad reached down and rubbed behind his ear, without taking his eyes from mine. "You're a funny lady, Sky Dylan Stone."

"Why do you say my whole name?"

"'Cause I wanna call you Sky. It fits you so well. If I called you Sky, would you answer?"

"We'd have to see," I said. He could call me Nanny-nanny-boo-boo and I would answer.

He stood up and gently pulled me off the car to my feet. He wrapped his arms around me, pressing the entire length of his body against mine. I could feel the heat of him through my clothes.

Hold back, my thinking brain warned. But I couldn't. I stood on tiptoe and reached up to his mouth as he leaned to kiss me again and we fit like puzzle pieces—my breasts just under the swell of his chest, the hard parts of him against the soft spots of me.

"Sky," he said, almost a groan, his mouth on mine. "The beautiful Sky..."

Restraint = zero.

The Sky wanted to melt, let her knees give way and flow to the ground.

But then he seemed to reel himself back in. *Damn!* He let

go of my body, slowly, so I wouldn't crumple. I got enough feeling back in my limbs to move them and rested against the car beside him. I lined up my leg next to his. My heart and my head were arguing as we stared out at nothing. I tried to figure out what he was fighting.

"We could go in," I suggested, to see if I could chase Silence away. No such luck. Finally, I asked, "What's the name of your company?" Admittedly, it was a pitiful attempt to keep him there. It wasn't as pathetic as throwing myself at his feet and hanging on to his ankle, which I also considered. I could feel him leaving me; he was all but gone.

Maybe it had been too much for him. Maybe he had felt me planning our golden years together. Sky Dylan Stone, Love Jinx Supreme.

After a minute or so he said, "Davis Construction."

Now what? I couldn't think. I looked down at his ankle. No. I'd have to let him go.

He looked over at me. "And buildingplans.com."

"Good names," I mumbled. And then another reasonable question occurred to me. "Are you going to take either one public?"

He sighed in the dark. "My Internet partners have start-up fever. But I'm being stubborn."

"Why? Doesn't everybody—everybody cool, anyway—want their own IPO? Isn't it unAmerican not to?" I asked, only half joking.

"I do. Someday, yeah. But we're not ready. Not yet."

"I see. You're a *haste = waste* guy," I said, trying anything to keep this conversation going, including sounding like an idiot.

"Hadn't thought of it like that. But sure, that sums it up."

Okay, Dylan. Shut up, now. Let it go. Let him *go if he wants.* My mouth opened anyway. "Sorry 'bout that. I think in formulas. My mom taught me to program in BASIC when I was really little and it's kinda crept into my brain patterns."

"Nah, it's great. It means you're logical and that's good. How would you say that? Logical = good?"

"No, I'd say that Logical = boring." Boy, did that sound like my mother or what?

He laughed. Thank goodness. So I kept pressing. "What about your construction company? Will you sell that when you make enough money with your Web pages?"

"No way. Davis Construction keeps us focused. We're always making improvements to the pages based on what we need on a job. It's why we're good. Essential content. Can you get what you want?"

I couldn't resist. I tried, but I'm weak. "You can't always get what you want," I sang, sounding not even a tiny bit like the Stones. We laughed together, mellow again. But he was gone. It was time to give up. He was a lot better at Restraint than I was. *At least I came up with a good exit song.* "I guess I better go in," I said, sounding quite cool and breezy, to my ears anyway. "I have to be up for a 6:30 breakfast meeting."

"Ooh." He winced, nodding. And didn't argue.

I hate Sunday weddings. Only the happy couple gets the next day off. Everybody else has to straggle back to their real lives.

Brad walked me and Guinness to the door and, under the oh-so-unromantic burglar-deterrent light with a squadron of moths flicking over our heads, he'd reached under my wild hair with his builder's hands and held my head so he could look in my eyes. I closed them so I wouldn't go blind. And, okay, for other reasons, too.

It's a good thing I didn't die after that first one because I hadn't *really* been kissed until his mouth sent twin jolts of electricity racing along the back of my throat, zinging down to my breasts, rousing sleeping nipples, meeting in a giant explosion between my legs. Or maybe it was an implosion because everything felt all tucked-up and tight. He covered my mouth with his, those velvet-cushion lips, and every neuron in my body screamed. Or maybe they were panting. I ached to melt into him, to have his body in mine.

As we parted, he said, "Nice to meet you, at last, Dylan Stone, Sky Dylan Stone." His lips brushed mine. "Sky."

Then he was gone, heading down the driveway. "I'll call," he said, without turning around, a final, weak attempt at Restraint. But I'd felt the fire beneath that facade. We were just too perfect together. *Rings and weddings and fortunes be damned. This has to be love.*

It wasn't until the next day that I stopped swooning long enough to remember that he hadn't asked for my phone number.

6

MONDAY MORNING HELL is a sales meeting on toast. Five straight hours of rah-rah, PowerPoint and positive thinking, all before lunch. Scary. This was my first real exposure to the M4: the Monthly Motivation Morning Marathon. I might have those words mixed up. It doesn't matter. To anyone. Maybe I wasn't cut out for sales. But then again, no one had ever bought me breakfast the whole time I was in programming.

I sat in the last row of the hotel meeting room, befitting my status as the newbie, and occupied myself with thoughts of Brad. His wonderful mind. His soulful eyes. Those kisses... I'd found true love while hanging upside down, exposing my teeny French thong to the world. *Cringe.* Please, don't think about that!

The guy up front was droning on. What insidious ploy had Microsoft used to get the world to use PowerPoint? Who thought people learned like this?

1. Stuff audience in dark room.

2. Speak in monotone.

3. Flash brightly colored, incomprehensible sentence fragments on faraway screen. Accompany with irritating sounds and fade-outs.

4. Ask for questions from survivors.

This month's marathon was a presentation about the effective use of PowerPoint as a sales tool. Shoot me.

Andie's right. Her job's better, I thought, *despite its obvious drawbacks.* Anything was better than this.

Andie worked for an agency called Talking Heads, Inc. They rented out talent for conventions, trade shows and the like. There were two kinds of talent: body—or booth babes—and voice. The booth babes wore bikinis or cat suits or schoolgirl uniforms to lure customers into the salesmen's lair. Unfortunately for world civilization, booth babes were highly effective. Andie was a voice talent, although they kept trying to talk her into wearing the short plaid skirt, tight white blouse and schoolbag.

Sometimes her audience would be standing just inches away—like at car shows—close enough to smell them. And some of the guys that go to those shows... You don't want to be that close. Andie usually wore serious, dark business suits and black pumps. Only the suits were way too short for a real office and the heels extra high. And she couldn't wear a blouse. The outfits resembled *Playboy*'s take on appropriate business attire. It was all fine with Andie. That's how she dressed anyway.

She'd do her stage-speak thing with the microphone, pulling her perfectly made up lips back from her little white teeth, rounding her vowels, enunciating carefully to get rid of her East Texas drawl.

"The Dodge Dakota's 5.9-liter, Magnum V-8 engine is capable of producing an impressive 345 pound-feet of torque at 3,200 rpm," she'd recite, standing beside the little truck on a huge turntable at the Convention Center's car show.

"Hey, baby," someone would holler, "how much power you packing under that hood of yours?"

Her incredible dark red hair would catch the light from the oversize bulbs, rippling and shining in time to her movements. "As you can see—" she'd make an expansive arm gesture "—this compact pickup sports a roomy cargo area."

"Your cargo area don't look so roomy. Looks tight, baby, nice and *tight*."

Maybe I'd stick with PowerPoint after all.

WHEN I GOT BACK to my office I had seven messages. The first was from a programmer in my old department who wasn't up on some of the advanced stuff we'd been doing before I left.

"Dylan," the voice mail said. "Your multimedia conferencing module is crap. You code like a girl." That was the kind of thing you said when you'd starved all those social areas of your brain.

I whizzed through the other six messages without listening to any of them. Eva—three, her fiancé—three, Brad—zero.

Sigh. It was too soon for him to call, but sigh anyway.

The six messages were all about the wedding, no doubt. The abyss. The inner ring of hell. Could we have some apocalyptic music down here, please? Wedding number twelve was at hand.

Eva, Andie and I had been best friends since we met in college. The three of us were a perfect fit: Andie from her shotgun shack, Eva from her historic San Antonio mansion and me from all over the place. What we most had in common were our wacko mothers and unavailable fathers. Except that couldn't have been the only thing or we'd have been friends with 99 percent of all other girls our age, too.

Now Eva was marrying Ron, aka Dr. Creep. I always got a cocktail of feelings thinking about it. But mostly I just felt sick. For Eva and me both. Which might sound like more wedding envy, but it wasn't. This wedding was a bad idea.

Three messages from Dr. Creep. It's supposed to be the

bride's mom who was difficult during the planning phase. But Eva's poor pill-popping mom wasn't lucid enough to stand up let alone push. I guess Ron felt he had to take charge, be obnoxious enough for both of them. Or, really, that's just who he was. He was probably calling to inform me of my myriad shortcomings as a wedding planner. And as a person.

"We don't need a wedding consultant," Eva had said to me when they'd first begun plotting this fiasco. "You only use those if you don't know what you want. But I know exactly what I want and who I want and where and when I want them. You can help me. You're one of those people that gets things done."

The classic master-slave relationship. Why hadn't I sweetly declined? Probably because it was so weird when Eva, the cloud dweller, got focused. It was like a mist lifting. It could take your breath away. As well as any good sense, apparently.

I wasn't ready to talk to Ron. My morning had been dismal and hadn't allowed for nearly enough Brad time. For enjoying this feeling, without all of those nasty blue rubber bands pinching my heart. I'd been right to trust him, to finally make that leap.

The phone rang and wishful thinking took over. *It's him!*

"Dyl, Ron here."

I was never going to answer a phone again.

"Hello, Ron." I had another name for him, of course, but it wasn't one of my nicer ones.

"You have to do something about Eva. She's upset and wants a different wedding dress. Call her."

"Ron! That's a Vera Wang! It was, what, six months in the making and remaking and the re-remaking? Plus it cost more than most cars. She can't change her mind now!"

"Don't be an ass," he exploded. "I *know* that! I paid for it, remember?" He calmed a bit. "That's why you have to call her."

I don't dislike people for no reason. Ron was no exception.

"I like calm, Ron. So what do you say?" I asked, in my sweet voice. Well, *I* thought it was sweet. "The next one who yells, loses. How about it?" No answer.

I didn't need this now. I wanted to remember the way Brad's arms looked in his rolled-up white sleeves. How the muscles...

"Let's be nice for Eva," I suggested. Still no answer.

I had a policy when I couldn't cope with stuff. Or didn't want to. I wrote a poem. On the computer of course. I don't know if I remembered how to hold a pen. It didn't help solve the problem, but it distracted me. Which was almost as good. Sometimes better. I stuffed the phone in the crook of my neck and began typing: *My best friend's wedding.*

Ron must have heard the keys clicking. "Dylan!" he yelled in my ear.

"Ron, you're screaming again. Does that mean I win?" Heavy breathing was the reply. "Ron? Just tell me what's wrong with the dress."

He growled. "It's too goddamn revealing."

"What does that mean?" I typed some more on my poem.

"What don't you understand?" Each word got louder. He stopped. More heavy breathing. "Get it, Dylan? She's hanging out. Her boobs—" He paused. "Eva feels her breasts are displayed too prominently."

"*Your* breasts." I might've forgotten to use my sweet voice.

"Dyl, I'm going to explain this to you," he said, lethally quiet now. I almost could hear his teeth grinding. "Eva is my fiancée. And I love her. She was concerned about the way the wedding dresses fit when she was first trying them on. You know that, you were there." His voice got clinical sounding. "She felt, as many women do, that her breasts were not adequate. We opted for surgical enhancement. She and I together. Doctor and patient."

"Yes, except it was *you* who felt her breasts were inadequate in those dresses. Eva lives in the clouds. She had never said a thing about her breasts until you suggested it. She did it to please you." I typed some more on my poem.

"We're not having *this discussion*," he shouted into the phone. "And you know what I think? You didn't want her to have surgery because you can't frigging stand competition. Especially from someone as classy as Eva. You wanted to rub it in her face. Didn't you? How flat she was. Or was it an accident that you tried on some of those same wedding dresses? Show her how much better you filled them out, how much better they looked on you." And then he got ugly. Uglier. "And you know what else? You blew it with Sean. He's bringing a real babe to the wedding. One who's not frigid. Tough luck all around, boob girl. You've lost Sean and Eva's tits are better than yours. And bigger. And they're *never gonna sag!*"

The phone banged down. I didn't get the receiver away from my ear in time. *Ow!* It was probably frustrating for Dr. Sphincter when he had to use his cell phone. Hard to get the same anger across just by pressing the End button.

Boob Girl?

Talk about ruining a mood. I sat there listening to the dial tone until I could breathe again. Then I finished my poem.

My best friend's wedding
a wedding for Eva = heaven
number of guests = too many to tell
number of bridesmaids = seven
an asshole groom = best friend's hell

Good thing I had other, more marketable, skills.

I thought about what The Sphincter had said. Not the boob thing. About Sean bringing someone else to the wedding. Sean was Ron's twin brother. The nice one. We'd double-dated a bit with Eva and Ron. Another one of those relationships I'd had that didn't go anywhere. Yesterday that might have been depressing. But now the jinx was broken. I had somebody real in my life. *His smile…*

My phone rang again. I felt like it was Matt. I *knew* it was Matt. What could he possibly want? Probably to ask me about Brad. Or talk about my thong.

Poor Matt. I should probably talk to him. He seriously was a nice guy who had been thrown off balance by Eva. More like crushed. Annihilated. He'd been engaged to Eva when she met Ron up in Dallas. And that was that. But she kept putting off jettisoning Matt. Poor Matt, the pale, the exhausted, the not much fun Matt who was in the throes of a brutal residency at the teaching hospital in Austin.

I remember one nasty Sunday afternoon when we were all hanging out at Skinny's in the big overstuffed chairs. Andie, Eva and I had intended to go to the lake until the weather reneged on its early promise. Matt had dragged in to meet us for a short break before he went back to his shift. We were all pretty drab, not just Matt.

Skinny's kept a supply of games for days like that. The shy and the socially inept found them useful for all occasions. Card games. Board games. Bored games. We were halfheartedly playing some stupid thing like Romantic Pursuits, and this question came up: Would you rather meet your soul mate after you've married someone else or not at all? You had only the two choices. a) After b) Never.

Andie chose c). She insisted that she was going to marry

her soul mate. No question. She would never, ever, ever marry anyone else. Since there was only one soul mate per person, she didn't have to worry about after. Problem solved. End of response.

If only life were that tidy. She hadn't met anyone even approximating soul mate potential. I didn't ask what she'd do if she found herself pushing an ancient thirty and he still hadn't showed. Why make the day grayer?

My turn was next. It doesn't take a clairvoyant to figure out what I'd said, true-believer that I was. A soul mate was a soul mate. You take 'em when and where you can get 'em.

"You mean you'd break up your family?" they all sputtered at once. "You'd ruin your kids? You'd throw everything away on a fling?"

I ran that through my processor and a revelation popped out. "What do you mean, ruin your kids?" I asked, realizing in one of my midchat epiphanies that I was the only one from a broken home. Well, not just broken. Make that compound-fractured. How weird. Their families had been so dismally dysfunctional that I hadn't focused on the fact that they were all still intact. Eva's used-to-be-successful dad and her bored, pill-popping mother. Andie's angry father and her listless mom with the black, vacant eyes and punching bag face. My family members might have been, as individuals, somewhat offbeat. A bit extraordinary, perhaps. But we were functional as a family, thank you very much. All of us. Sometimes even some of the exes and the steps. Well, not the current step, but the rest of us. Well, some of the rest of us. "I'm not ruined!"

Eva and Andie didn't say anything. Just looked at me. It was a bleak, bitchy day and those were some smug expressions on their faces.

Matt broke in. "I agree with Andie." He reached across the big padded arm of his chair for Eva's left hand and squeezed it, rubbing her engagement ring with his finger. "I've found my soul mate," he said, pressing his lips into her palm. He let his eyes feast on her fragile face and dark halo of curls. "And nothing will ever change that."

Eva turned from staring at me to look at Matt, her hard face unaltered. It would have been nice, right then, to slither out the front door and slip quietly into the rain. I was an unreformed Avoider. This was not going to be fun.

"Really? *C'est vrai?*" she said, and slid on her not-of-this-world, delicate face. Which was a good thing. The other one was pretty scary. Her tone got dreamy, but her words didn't soften. "I don't believe in soul mates. You know? Things change. Look at all the unhappy married people. You think they knew it would turn out like that?" She moved her hand out of Matt's, stuffed it between her thighs and looked at each one of us. Nobody breathed. We could feel the ground shifting. Especially Matt. "No," she said, answering herself. *"Pas de tout.* Of course not." She sighed and looked off to the side, far away. Probably all the way to Ron's Dallas mansion. "I think the best thing is to find someone you're compatible with. Someone who can give you a comfortable life."

Matt got even paler. Matt, with his okay earning prospects, was not in the league that she required. Eva was a Toppo; she needed more than Matt could give her. Lots more.

When she and I first met, it took me a long time to understand that about Eva. It was a concept so foreign to me that I could never quite get my brain to accept it. Evalina Aguirre-Velasquez—two parts Spanish, two parts French— was all parts Toppo. Toppos were people who said stuff such as, "Look what I bought. You wouldn't believe how much I had to pay! It's top of the line. Absolute top of the line." Toppos *liked* to overpay. Always. For everything. When the value ratio got all out of whack and Ms. Cost was way too top-heavy for Mr. Benefit, they knew they had gotten hold of something special.

I used to think Eva was pretty weird but she'd introduced me to a whole bunch of folks just like her: people who pay too much. What a revelation for someone like me who got more zing from the afterglow of a good deal than from the thing I bought.

Eva had just informed Matt that she needed a comfortable life. I had the uncharitable thought that it would take one hellacious bank-load of cash to keep this Toppo comfy.

"And you know what else I think?" she turned her unfocused stare back on me and didn't wait for an answer. "If you're not unrealistic in your expectations then you won't be disappointed and end up miserable." Her eyes drilled straight into mine.

I am not unrealistic! I adore real.

Then she gave another big sigh. "Voilà! That's what I think."

I got up the nerve to glance over at Matt. His face looked like that of a patient just waking up from surgery. One who had discovered his doctors had cut off both his legs instead of taking out his tonsils. Poor guy. He'd found his soul mate and she was shopping for a lifestyle. I hoped I never saw a face like that again.

After Matt left, we all just sat there a minute. A little shaky from the vibes. "Voilà," said Eva.

"Don't start with the French, Eva," Andie groused. "I've already got a headache."

"Phhh," Eva shrugged and blew out a little French puff of air at Andie. Eva was two generations removed from her French roots, but her family used to go to Provence every summer when she was little so she could brush up on her Gallic ways. It seemed to me like she had 'em down pat.

"All in all, that went pretty well," Andie said to me. "I

doubt it'll come as much surprise when she gets around to giving him back his ring. He'll already have jumped by then."

I didn't answer, just kept seeing Matt's stricken face.

Eva didn't say anything, just stared down at Matt's ring on her hand. "What else could I do?" she asked quietly, talking more to herself. Then she straightened in her chair. "But I've found what I want," she said looking back and forth between Andie and me for validation. She didn't get it. We'd already met Ron.

Eva sucked on her finger to get Matt's engagement ring off. She held it in her hand, looking at it.

"I think it's sweet," Andie said. What did they used to call that? Damning with faint praise.

"It's teeny," Eva sighed, looking out the window. Probably trying to see the ring that Ron would give her. "Maybe Matt never really loved me."

"Why would you say that, Eva?" I asked, feeling totally appalled. "Matt adores you. He lives for you. He'd die for you."

"It's so tiny," she said, holding it up to the light.

This was too much. Even for Princess Top-of-the-Line. "He's a resident!" I was almost yelling and the Skinny's crowd noticed. I tried whispering instead. "What do you want? Do you even know how lucky you are? Having somebody love you like that."

Eva glanced at me, a worry flitting over her beautiful face. "Oh, Dylan. You're so idealistic. You can't be like this, so romantic and everything. You're gonna get hurt."

"She's not going to get hurt," Andie said, sticking up for me as usual.

I smiled my smug smile at Eva.

"She's never, ever going to let anybody get that close."

I gave Andie a look. "What's that got to do with Matt's

ring?" I asked, deflecting their concern for my love life. I didn't like to talk about it. It was pretty bleak. Back then.

"Guys can always get the money for a decent ring," Andie explained, as though I was just stupid. "If they care enough. It shows how much they love you." Another irrefutable fact. She settled all the way back in the big chair. Her feet didn't quite reach the floor. "I," she proclaimed, "am gonna find me a soul mate and he's gonna give me the biggest damn ring in the world. Because that's how much he's gonna love me."

I wasn't going to sway either Diamond Girl on that point. But what if carats didn't come with a soul mate attached? What if you had to trade love for diamonds?

"Are you sure about all this, Eva?" I asked. "You and Matt were so perfect." It wasn't that I thought Prudence was the greatest guy ever. He was a little—what's the word?—*constricted* for my taste. But Eva had loved him and he had loved her. If that wasn't real, then what in the world was?

"Ron is everything I've always wanted," Eva said, off again with the faraway gazing. Eva had only two modes of operation: cloud hovering and laser-focus. She usually preferred the clouds unless she had to come down to earth to get what she wanted. "I always knew I was going to marry a doctor." That's what you did in Eva's family. If you couldn't be a doctor, you married one.

"Matt's a doctor," Andie and I said together.

Eva rolled her eyes. Matt was on the wrong side of an invisible line. The idealistic side. The guy was working on a specialty in AIDS, not your typical high-income specialty. Eva, Toppo-supreme, was perched as far away as she could get from that line. Over there with the pragmatists.

"Ron has got a great practice," Eva explained to us, as if Andie and I hadn't already been apprised of The Practice. About a quadrillion times. "He's the best plastic surgeon up there, and you know how much those Dallas women have done. Something every six months. It's huge." She contemplated that, visibly moved by the immensity. "And," she added, "he's mature."

"Believe it," Andie laughed. "How old's his boy again? Eighteen? Nineteen? You gonna be stepmama to a dude just a few years younger than you? I'd say the old boy's mature."

"It doesn't matter," Eva shrugged. "None of that stuff does. We'll figure it out. I'm just so sick of guys who don't know what they want, don't know how to go out and get it. Ron can give me the things I need. That's what it all comes down to, really, what your life will be like. I mean, think about it. Do you want to work after you have kids?" she asked.

Andie and I shook our heads in unison. Eva had a point. Girls our age weren't into that whole liberation thing like our moms had been. From our perspective—the ones left alone, the turnkey kids—it hadn't worked out all that well.

"That's what's most important," Eva said. "What kind of stuff you'll be able to do. Otherwise, you'll be so miserable you can't stand it and you'll end up hating your husband."

"It sounds pretty soulless," I said.

"It's not," Eva said, giving me another of her pitying looks. "It's life. There are no soul mates, Dylan. No Prince Charmings. Just bills. And if you guys aren't careful you're going to end up old and single. And all alone." She might as well have slapped us. Old + single = fate worse than death.

Things had sure changed in the year since then. Twelve weddings for one thing. And now Brad. The charming Mr. Davis. My office phone stopped ringing. I watched for the message light, but Matt didn't leave one. If it was Matt, which I was still pretty sure it was. Unless it was Brad and

I'd just ignored a call from my soul mate, the one man in the entire universe who was right for me.

But it couldn't have been Brad. He would have left a message. Wouldn't he?

7

BRAD CALLED ME Monday afternoon—an entire, interminable week later. He'd had to look up my work number and that was a good sign, some small effort had been expended. But it'd taken him too long to pick up the phone. Two hundred and twelve hours to be exact. During that time, I'd gotten about three hours sleep.

If I'd believed in the tea leaves of dating, I would have said his call was a mixed signal. Mildly interested, perhaps, but not excited. Three days would have been more encouraging. That said eager, but not desperate. Except when you knew that this guy was the right one and it was the first time in your whole twenty-four befuddled years of life that that had ever happened, anything past an hour was cruel. And unusual. And damn near unforgivable.

That yearlong week had given most of me time to go back to being the old me. The Jinx. The rubber-banded me. Only a small part of Wishful held out. When I finally got Brad's message, I was too battle-weary to call back. I'd been fighting myself all week. *How could you be so stupid?* But he seemed so right! *What, you could tell that after a handful of kisses?* I know, but remember what they felt like? Wishful eventually won the debate, but when I called, I missed him. He was gone for the day. I left my cell number in my message so he could phone me anytime.

His next message didn't arrive until Friday—five, count 'em, five endless days—and it included both his home and cell phone numbers. That was an excellent sign and, had I not spent the prior week turned inside out, I might have been encouraged. But I knew by then where things stood. I was good at this kind of thing—the kind that went nowhere. I just needed to get myself together before I returned any phone calls.

So I spent the weekend with Eva, looking for a solution to her wedding dress boobs, I mean blues. It was just like the old days, prewedding, when we laughed and talked and forgot our real lives.

I could almost breathe by Monday and then, out of nowhere, an e-mail popped up in my list. I didn't recognize the address but the subject line said, "Sky, please don't forget me."

Wedding number eleven had been a lifetime ago. Or, really, three hundred and eighty heartbreaking hours ago. I'd spent the weekend putting the rubber bands neatly back in place around my heart. I sat at my desk, looking at that line and didn't know if I could read the message.

But then Wishful pictured his laughing eyes and his off-center grin. What would his e-mail say? What could it possibly say to make things right? I clicked it open.

"Too busy to breathe," it said. "More later."

I read it a hundred times as if those simple words were code for something. And something magical started to happen somewhere around the seventy-fifth time through. I could feel a couple of the rubber bands popping off. Wishful sighed. *I knew he cared, I just knew it!* Wishful was starving— any dry little morsel would do.

So we started e-mailing each other. He usually sent his sometime after 2:00 or 3:00 in the morning. A moral for the millennium: If you bite off more than you can chew, you'll probably choke. I told myself to be grateful he found any energy at all, trying to keep the flicker between us alive. I didn't *feel* particularly grateful. I wanted his strong arms around me. I wanted more kisses. I needed to be part of his life. His messages stayed dismally short. He wasn't just consumed with his work; it had already devoured him.

When we finally hooked up on the phone, we were almost strangers. It's always weird to stumble backward in a relationship, to go from hot and heavy to how do you do? All right, we hadn't been heavy exactly, but this was not the direction I'd dreamed of. We talked about his work and my work and mutual friends and mutual funds and anything else we could think of to fill the empty airspace.

He told me a little about his sister, Emily, so I got to talk about Asia and Greyson, too. But we didn't talk about that night or about *us*. The worst thing was he didn't seem to make any distinction between his work and his personal life. At best he was distracted, other times distant. Once in a while, I felt as if he was putting out the vibe, but where was there room in that life of his? Where in his hectic world was there space for love?

Even Wishful was about to give up and then the wildflowers began. I'd get back from a meeting or lunch and there they'd be. Fragile autumn-colored bouquets that brought meadows and sunshine into my drab, little world. They never lasted more than a day or two but Wishful wouldn't let me think of them as metaphor. I just buried my face in their fragrance and let Wishful do the thinking.

"This thing's all about content," he said during one of those times we actually got to talk to each other, infusing the techno-gibberish with his slow Texas rhythms. I loved it, the techie talk *and* the accent. "And the intersection of mediums through broadband. There's some fantastic up-side potential. We're in a strong position, but we've got to exploit the possibilities, find a way to..."

It was a lazy Sunday afternoon. I was alone in the apartment; Andie was out scouting soul mates. I'd been drying off from my post-run shower when the phone rang. I hobbled into a pair of panties with one hand and grabbed the phone with the other. I sat down sideways in one of our comfy chairs, all but naked, listening to his voice and watching a golden shaft of light cut through the front window. My bare legs were hanging over the arm and if I kicked them, I made the dust specks caught in the beam rise and swirl.

What was it he'd just said? Maybe I was *too* comfy. Had he asked me a question? I rewound it in my mind. Something about broadbands. I squirmed around a little in my chair and decided I'd better ask him my question. I'd been feeling the undercurrent again, that electric connection between us. Was Wishful doing my thinking? Surely it would be okay to just ask. I'd practiced the perfect tone in my head for days. Lighter than air.

"Would you go to another wedding with me?" Ms. Helium asked.

I'd waited too long. He'd started talking again at the exact same time. Silence. Then we both tried again. Silence again.

"You go ahead," I said, chickening out.

"No, no, it's okay." Silence was suddenly very noisy, lots of dead air. I could almost hear him rewinding his own tape. Then he asked, "What did you just say?"

"Um, nothing, nothing. Go on, what were you saying?"

"Did you just ask me to have a wedding with you?"

I laughed. Easily and naturally. Or that was my intention. "No," I chuckled. "You must be projecting again." Sometimes I wasn't as funny as I intended. Lots of times, actually. And we both knew there was no good response to that. *Good one, Dylan.*

"What *did* you say?" he asked.

Here goes. "I asked if you'd go to a wedding. With me."

I counted the beats with Silence: one potato, two potato,

three potato... Wedding talk was going to have significant impact on any guy's response time. I waited.

"Um, what wedding?"

After all that response time, it wasn't quite the response I was hoping for. "Does that matter?" Trying to be light again.

One potato, two potato...

"Yeah, maybe... No, I guess it really doesn't," he said, with palpable lack of enthusiasm. "Is it down there?"

"No. Number twelve's up by you. In Dallas. Next weekend."

"Number twelve?" he asked. Finally, a reasonable response.

"Yeah. Weddings-to-date," I said.

"Was that number eleven, where I met you?"

"Yeah. It was. And I have to be a bridesmaid again. Worse, the maid of honor. I think I'm gonna jump."

"Can't be that bad. You looked incredible the last time," he said, with just enough heat to make me think he meant it.

The sunbeam crept its way up my legs. I wasn't going to ask him again. Silence played more games. I was too exposed. I grabbed a throw off the couch and wrapped it around me.

"I don't think I'll be in town next weekend, Dylan," he said, not sounding particularly felled by disappointment.

Hey, what happened to Sky?

"Planning on having a headache?" I asked, softly, knowing how it sounded but not being able to stop myself. This wedding was making me crazy. No way I could go to the thing alone.

"I'm sorry," he said. He sounded as if he meant it.

What, is he finally going to invest a bit of himself in this conversation?

"I'd like to go. Well, maybe not *like*, I really don't care for weddings very much. But I *would* go. With you."

I pondered that. The man doesn't like weddings. I concentrated on the positive points of honesty.

"But I have to work," he continued.

"On the weekend?" I asked, as if I didn't work most weekends myself. Not even a girlfriend and already I was a nag.

"Yeah. This is important. I've got to go to South Carolina. One of my partners is trying to arrange a golf game—on Hilton Head—with a couple of big construction companies we're pitching. They're gonna be there for a conference and we're trying to catch 'em on neutral turf."

My life was over. No Brad. No date for Eva's wedding. I couldn't believe I hadn't done something about this earlier. The truth was I couldn't stand the thought of being with anyone but Brad. How stupid was that? Hanging on for Mr. Detached Davis of Dallas. Hadn't weeks of nothing given me a hint? I felt myself falling through all twelve circles of Dante's hell. Or however many he had.

I knew Brad wasn't lying; he probably did have to work. He was probably going to have to work every second of every day for the rest of his life. *This,* I thought as one more blue rubber band attached itself to my heart, *was just not meant to be.* "That's okay," I said with a little more sigh than I'd intended.

"I'm really sorry," he said.

"No, no. It's fine," I lied.

"Are you sure?"

"Mmm-hmm."

"This meeting could give us the break we need," he said, merrily picking up the conversation right where I'd interrupted. "Allow us to…"

I don't even remember getting off the phone.

My policy was to deal with the disappointments of life with immediate, unthinking overreaction. So now what? Who could I call? Matt was out. You don't invite the bride's ex to her wedding. Well, my mom always did, but nobody else would.

Sean was out. Dr. Sphincter had said he was bringing some babe to the wedding. *Why doesn't that bother me?* Sean and I had had fun the few times we went out. Until I met Brad, I'd just assumed Sean and I would go to the wedding together. Best man and maid of honor. Good symmetry. So what did I think of Sean's defection? Not a thing.

I should write a poem. But I didn't have the energy to sit at my computer. So now what? No Brad, no Matt, no Sean, no dates. And an unending procession of weddings. I slid to the floor and put my face to my knees. There was a joke in there somewhere. Except my funny lobe had shut itself off.

Why was it so hard for me? Everybody else had somebody. Well, everybody but Matt. Couples one through twelve had each other. Sean had some new hottie. Andie always had some big guy hanging around. Brad had his work. My eyes began to sting.

I took a big breath and lifted my head. *This is unacceptable*, the rational side of me thought. *You are not going to feel sorry for yourself.*

Okay, so I'd be logical. Analyze why this whole love thing was so hard for me. I started with Brad. I saw his mouth first, then his eyes and the rest of him materialized in my head. Brad. The guy I'd never really had but still had managed to lose.

See, Dylan, my rational lobe said. *You're not thinking straight. You can't lose a guy you never had.*

But what happened? I asked myself. *He'd seemed so right. What did I do to jinx it?*

The Brad in my head turned and looked at me the way he had before the last kiss. As if he was falling in love, too.

The only trouble with Brad, Rational said, *is that he's too busy. And he's so damn overworked it may never be right. Give it up.*

Except, I love thinking about him. I could see him standing there, his arms straight out, asking Groom Daddy to dance.

You're dreaming, Rational answered. I felt her logical fist on my heart. *Give him up.*

Rational was right. Brad was always going to be too busy. Always just out of reach. I couldn't quite catch my breath. It might have been easier if I had just let myself cry. I scooted down flat on the cool floor and lay there on my back, looking up at the ceiling, trying not to whimper.

It seemed that other girls managed to find happiness, to live the dream. I was going to be the shriveled crone in the corner with no life of my own. I'd make hateful remarks about diamonds, stirring my jealous ashes.

Okay, how about Matt? I asked myself. *He was interested in me before number eleven. Until I ran him off.*

The thought of that stopped me for a second. Was that what I did? Run from guys who wanted me and long for the ones who didn't? I mulled that over awhile. No, that wasn't right, either. Matt didn't want me; he wanted Eva. Good enough reason to run.

So maybe it was like Eva said. I needed to get practical. Quit looking for love and start searching for diamonds. *And end up with a guy like Ron?* I asked myself.

Thanks, but no. I turned over and lay on my side, rolled up in a ball, with my knees tucked up under my chin. Guinness plopped down beside me and gave the side of my face an occasional lick of concern.

I don't know how long I stayed curled up like that. My only sense of passing time were sporadic wet slurps.

It was dark and cold in the room when I finally opened my eyes. From this angle I could see all of the dust balls under the furniture. *Jeez*, I told myself as I sat up, *get a grip*. Guinness sat beside me and leaned his solid chocolate torso into mine.

"Let's see," I said to him, trying to focus on the upcoming week. Anything to forget the pinching in my chest. "It's Sunday. Four days to go on the countdown to hell." Guinness agreed or at least he laid his head on my arm.

The itinerary for number twelve—wedding of the year, no egregious excess spared—required that I leave my cozy Austin hideout and show up in the ritzy center of Dallas on Thursday for Eva's final shower and the formal kickoff of the festivities. That evening we were having the out-of-town guests' dinner. The rehearsal was on Friday and the big day was on Saturday.

The good thing—the *only* good thing—was that my mom lived just outside of Dallas. My plan was to drive up after work on Wednesday and stay with her throughout the ordeal. I was determined to spend quality time with my family, no matter what. Their loving company would restore me, and render me fit to face the difficult days ahead.

8

THERE'S LOTS TO BE SAID about being the daughter of a flower child, but all I cared about as I pulled my Jeep up in front of my mom's house in Suburbanville, Texas, on that Wednesday night—four hours later than expected—was getting one of her world-class hugs. She came running out of the house before I'd fully stopped, yanked my door open and dragged me down from my seat. Without a word, I stood and rested my head against hers and let her pump her spirit into my wilting aura. You couldn't be Leila's kid and not know about auras, and she could tell mine needed a recharge. I'd been looking forward to this wedding about as much as having my toenails removed, but after only a few moments in that healing embrace I was beginning to think that maybe things wouldn't be so bad after all.

Leila lived in a colossal stone home on a cul-de-sac in Suburbanville, the *in* Dallas suburb. It was a most un-Leila-like location. She and her latest husband had moved there after I graduated from high school. This life was her ninth or tenth incarnation—just since I'd been counting. She was happy now. But then Leila was always happy. She'd put us through seven kinds of hell making certain of it.

In this life, she owned her own painting business: Fantasy Faux. She created some of the most awesome walls in Dallas with the weirdest stuff—sea creatures, T-shirts, chicken wire, old newspapers. Her walls were in such demand that she'd had to hire three crews just to keep up. She had them do the background work, then she'd come in and do the magic.

"Leila, are you staying out there all night?" We jumped at my stepfather's voice. Like ice crackling. "Dylan," he turned his chill on me, "you have a call."

I was yanked from my mother's arms and hurled through ominous black clouds and frigid air to land with a thud in step-hell. It's a lot like the other hell, except here you don't burn. You ice over. The step-freeze.

Hello, Grant, I said in my head to his gray-blond buzz cut. *How delightful to see you again.*

Grant McKay worshipped Leila, adored his son, Grey, and his adopted daughter, Asia, and thought of me as a living, breathing viral attack. The uninvited guest, difficult to ignore, impossible to get rid of. I thought of him as Step Away.

I'd dreamed his name right after my little brother was born. I must have been about sixteen. In my dream, Leila and Asia were standing in an empty parking lot; Leila had a baby in her arms. They were absolutely still, everything eerily quiet. I was floating toward them—the way you do in dreams—reaching out with both arms for the baby and just when I started to get close, a roar came out of the dark behind me. I froze. Leila clutched the baby high on her chest and little Asia started to scream, a shrill, piercing screech that went on and on. I couldn't look behind me, knowing whatever was there was going to be awful. But I felt myself turning anyway and, a safe distance away, Grant stood with a bullhorn to his mouth. I could hear his words. "Step away from the baby. Do you hear me? Put down your arms and step away from the baby." I turned back to Leila, but they were gone.

"Leila? Are you coming in?" Step Away demanded again.

As Leila and I walked up to the house, I asked, "Hey! Where are the kids?"

Grant answered as he turned into the house. "It's late. Where do you think? You could have called."

Except I couldn't. My cell phone was dead and I'd forgotten the charger. But he was right about me being late. I couldn't get out of the office. I'd been trying to do some damage control with a sale I was about to lose on the West Coast. It appeared now that they'd been stringing me along, pretending they were interested but never really intending to buy our services. Instead, they pumped us for all the free information they could get—requests for preliminary evaluation services and initial requirements analysis. I'd been cooperating, betting on the big deal. A less-than-propitious start on the new sales career.

"Get the phone in the kitchen," Step Away said. God forbid I should use the one right there next to me in his office.

Brrrr! I was a specialist on step-freeze, intimate with its frost line. There wasn't a cold shoulder or a chilly reception, an icy stare or a frigid refusal that I hadn't been exposed to. I was born a child of divorce, literally. My mother and father were already split up when I was conceived. In fact, if I understand the chronology correctly, Leila was living with another guy when the inconvenient conception by her ex-husband occurred. The other guy must have been out of town or distracted for a minute or something. Anyway, Leila and my dad decided that the only solution to my imminent birth would be for them to remarry. Life was tough enough. They didn't want to saddle me with any legitimacy concerns. Plus they really liked each other. And, knowing my mom, it seemed like a good idea at the time.

Leila left her current love, remarried my dad and moved back in. A year or so after I was born, trouble began to brew again in the happy household. Leila and my dad remembered why they'd gotten divorced in the first place—they couldn't get along for any extended period of time, not in the same house. So just before I was two, they got divorced again.

With a single bounce on the rebound, Leila got back with the other guy and promptly married him. That, too, probably seemed liked a good idea. Not quite two and—ta da!—I had my first official stepfather. I have just a few memories of Step One, but they're sharp ones. I know he resented me. I was, after all, the cause of his losing Leila, twice. He never said much, but he broadcasted over the vibe lines loud and clear. "Go away. Please, just...go...away."

Eventually, Leila left him. Outrage was the only thing that could have propelled us out of our beloved New Mexico into the badlands of Texas. It wasn't right for New Mexicans to move to Texas. We were supposed to despise the state and every skiing, boating, hunting, fishing, hiking, camping, turquoise-collecting, hat-wearing, boot-stomping, loud-talking, dumb-sounding person in it. Hence the unofficial state motto: Poor New Mexico, so far from God, so close to Texas.

"We're not going to put up with *that*," Leila had huffed as we started out on the journey east, slamming the palms of her hands on the steering wheel. "We are a team, you and I. We don't come separately packaged. Damn him!" Leila was a charter member of the love-me-love-my-kid club. Well, until the advent of Step Away, that is. Then she'd had to give up her membership and settle for two out of three.

When I risk a little sled-ride down memory lane and reminisce about the other Step Freezers, I see just how good I had it with Step One. His chill was more like a stiff breeze than the subarctic blizzards I got to shiver in later. Of course, that happens to me a lot, realizing later that something was a lot better than I thought at the time.

As I wound my way through Leila's big house to her kitchen, I worked on a plan to keep Step Away from freezing me out this time. *Think warm thoughts. Mocha lattes, blue corn enchiladas, nipple-zinger kisses.* And then I knew. It was Brad on the phone.

"Hey," he said. He always materialized in my head like the Cheshire cat. Mouth first.

"Where are you?" I asked. *At work,* Rational answered. *Where do you think?*

"Here."

"Where's that?"

"Dallas."

"You are!" *Hallelujah.* I always forgot to be cool when it counted. "Um, how did you know where to reach me?" I asked, cool as could be in an effort to counterbalance the hallelujah.

"Eva gave me your mom's number."

"Eva? You know Eva?"

"No, but I called Andie at your house and she was being so loyal she couldn't decide if it was okay to give me the number. I couldn't accept that so she called Eva to see what she thought and Eva called me and gave it to me. But nobody volunteered to call over there and talk to your stepfather themselves."

And could you blame them?

"Listen," he said. "I've been thinking. I could leave early Friday instead of tomorrow. We could spend all day together."

Wow! Where was Detached Brad, the one who couldn't squeeze a phone call into his schedule?

"Yeah, okay," I said. *Are you mad?* Rational screamed.

He started to say something else when I continued saying, "Except there's a problem." I explained about the wedding stuff I had to do.

"No way you could get out of it?" he asked, not understanding at all about weddings. "Just for a few hours?"

"I am so sorry."

"But I have the whole day! That may never happen again."

There was nothing I could say. I couldn't miss Eva's stupid shower—her seventh.

"Damn," he said, and then lowered his voice to the leading-man rumble. "Well. What about tonight?"

"Now? It's almost eleven!"

"So? I need to see you, Sky." I loved that rumbley voice, the one I'd had such a hard time resisting in the first place. Okay. I wasn't really trying. And I was back to being Sky. That had to mean something!

"I thought you'd get in earlier," he continued talking. "I couldn't get you on your cell. I've been leaving messages all over the place. Calling, bugging your stepfather. He hates me."

It didn't seem like he was worried about being cool, either. I spun around on one foot and there was said stepfather, glaring. And I'd just been about to tell Brad that it wasn't him Step Away hated. Anything remotely connected to me just made the man irritable. That's why Andie and Guinness had to stay somewhere else, with other friends.

"Earth to Sky. Come in, please. Can you meet me?"

I thought I'd already said yes. Maybe I was getting a little too friendly with Silence. I kept forgetting to talk. "Okay," I said, turning my back on Step Away. We agreed to meet at the local all-night Pancake House. This was, after all, Suburbanville. It was either there or Wal-Mart.

"I guess I'm going to meet Brad for coffee," I told Leila as I got off the phone.

Step Away jumped in. "That's great. Your mother's been waiting all night. Standing there at the window. Worrying!"

"No. No, Grant. It's fine," Leila laughed, reaching up to stroke his face with the side of her finger. "I *want* her to go. I think we might like this guy." She smiled at me. I could do no wrong in Leila world.

"It's not fine, it's selfish," Grant grumped.

And so we encountered the very core of Step Freeze: The Glacial Sea of Resentment. When I was a teenager, I used to think that he just considered me a poor investment, a money pit. I could see the suffering that each financial or emotional outlay cost him. Dylan = black hole.

I thought our relationship would improve once I was out of his house, self-sufficient, independent. But if anything, things had gotten worse between us. I realized that it wasn't a drain of resources that he resented. I was a drain on his family's affections. Every scrap of love and caring I received from them was stolen directly from him. Dylan = rival.

It was funny, well not *funny*, but I always looked forward to coming and visiting Leila and the kids with such naive anticipation, as if each time I thought it would be different. And each time, after ten minutes in the deep freeze, I was desperate to leave.

9

BRAD WAS WAITING for me in the parking lot and he walked over to my Jeep as soon as I pulled in. He opened my door, offered his hand to help me down and kept my hand in his as we stood toe to toe under the bright lights. I wasn't sure who I was meeting—the incredibly romantic fellow who had rescued me from Groom Daddy's clutches and called me Sky or the stressed-out, preoccupied entrepreneur who barely remembered my name.

He smiled into my face, moved a few of my curls aside with his other hand, and stroked my cheek, exactly like Leila's soothing touch of Step Away's cheek back in Step-Hell. While I pondered the significance of that, he cupped my chin, leaned down and kissed the top of my forehead. Apparently this was the first Brad.

We had walked into the restaurant, sat across from each other, ordered and gotten our coffee before he let go of my hand.

"I've missed you," he said from across the sticky Formica.

I took a sip of decaf paint thinner. Skinny's had spoiled me rotten, no other coffee tasted good anymore.

Be cool, Jinx, I told myself. *Try not to blow it this time.* "Do you have a twin?" I asked. Clearly that was Jinx talking.

"What do you mean?" he said with a questioning kind of laugh.

"Well, it seems to me—" I tried for that perfect tone of voice that says, "I'm not easy" "—that you must be the guy

I met at a wedding a while back. But if that's true, then who's the guy I've been talking to for the last few weeks? You can't be the same person, so I'm assuming you have an evil twin. Or maybe you're a multiple."

"A multiple?" he asked.

"DID. Dissociative Identity Disorder. Formerly known as Multiple Personality Disorder." I said it laughing but inside I was cursing, wondering what in the hell I was talking about. "It sounds like I know a lot about this stuff, huh?" He must have thought I was nuts.

He nodded—eyebrows up, eyes wide and his grin in its usual off-center location.

Oh, good. It didn't look like Jinx had scared him off yet.

"Don't worry. I talk to myself all the time, but I know I'm doing it. So which is it? Evil twin or multiple?"

His brow crinkled up nicely. "Yeah, I mean, no. I mean, sorry about that." He sighed. "Man, it's been insane." He paused and grunted out a little laugh. "Not as in 'Dissociate Identity Disorder' but as in I need ten of me to get everything done." He reached for my hand again. "But, Sky, I've been thinking about you. A lot. I couldn't stand the thought of you being here so close and me not seeing you." He paused again, then served up a slow-roasted grin. "And I wouldn't have said it was possible, but you look even better than I remembered."

You are not in love with this guy, Dylan, Rational groused. *Remember? He won't be ready to settle down until you're old and barren.*

I looked at his burnt-toast eyes drilling into mine. "Thank you," I said, trying to sound all earnest and intense, hoping he wouldn't notice the rubber bands hitting the floor. *Cool, Dylan. Be cool.*

Maybe Rational was right. Maybe I should try to resist this guy. I forced myself to not look at his mouth, but his eyes weren't any safer. And as I stared at them, I could feel a lightness in my chest.

Of course I'm right. Just look at him! The guy's a rocket. You think he's going to cool his jets any time soon? The longer I stayed single, the more emotional Rational seemed to get. If she wasn't careful, I was going to have to rename her.

"But let's look at this logically," I mumbled. I freed my hand and started to trace a flow chart on the table using the water ring from my glass as ink. When in doubt, act nerdy, I always say. I drew the chart upside down so it would make sense from his side.

"We started here," I said and sketched a little tent. "And, I don't know about you, but it was a good thing for me. Meeting you made me happy." I put a smiley face inside the tent—one with lots of curly hair—and made sunrays fanning out behind it. "Now, for almost a month, in all our various forms of communication—" I drew an arrow from the tent and several little connecting boxes; some boxes pointed to other boxes, but most were dead ends with little Xs crossed through them "—you have displayed not one modicum of emotion. Flat line. Zip. So this is what I don't get." I stuck a circle at the bottom of my chart on his side of the table. "You're sitting here all warm and accessible—" I put a smiley face in the circle "—and it's like the last month never happened. We're back to the first night we met."

I put a big X over all of the little boxes, drew a big heart around the face and made a line coming down to it, directly from the tent at the top. I looked at him as he studied the chart, as if there was something to learn there, some hidden secret in it.

"Don't bother," I said to him. "None of it makes any sense." I took my paper napkin and wiped the flow chart away. The table was significantly less sticky when I was done. I folded the napkin and put my hands in my lap.

He looked up at me, straight-faced. "I thought you said logical = boring."

"I lied." A guy who not only listens but remembers? What were the odds? Jeez, he was good-looking. Or maybe it was the fact that he wasn't gorgeous—just a guy who happened to have a great grin and mysterious eyes. That was his appeal. "It's not that I'm not flattered. 'Cause I am. I like it that you wanted to see me tonight. But I have to know what's up. It makes me a tad uneasy when things aren't what they seem."

"A tad?" he repeated.

"Yeah. Maybe even more than a tad."

"What? Like a smidgen?"

"This is not helping," I said.

"Okay. Truth?"

"Please."

"It's complicated," he hedged.

"That's okay. I like complicated."

"More coffee?" he asked.

I'd hardly touched my first cup of acid. I lifted my eyebrows at him and waited.

He heaved another big sigh. "I really did need to see you tonight... Do you want something to eat?"

I blinked.

"That was a pretty good logic chart. I bet you were a dynamite programmer," he said.

And I waited some more.

So, finally, he launched into this concise, well-organized account of another woman. I almost flew out the double glass doors in front I was so blown away. I had never, ever, not for one nanosecond, thought about there being someone else. I'd been thinking that the explanation for the two Brads was that he was one of those people who was more comfortable with face-to-face encounters. He just needed to see me in person. That was all. Or maybe, I thought, he'd finally gotten a breather at work and had time to focus on me again. As though I was finally granted priority in his needs hierarchy.

I'd been just fishing, waiting for him to say how he'd had an epiphany, that he'd discovered he was ready to get serious, spend time together, have a more balanced life. During our entire flurry of electronic correspondence, I had never once felt anyone else there with us. It was my turn to sigh. *Maybe I'm no good at reading digital vibes,* I thought. Maybe there were no digital vibes.

Mentally slack-jawed, I sat there and listened as he explained to me that one of his partners in the Internet business was a hottie with whom he'd been involved at a prior job. They'd loved hard and then split up when she'd dumped him for their boss at the time. Brad had left, looking for something more concrete or stable and had ended up buying his construction company. When he was ready to create his own Internet presence, he'd asked her to help them out. Apparently she did dynamite interfaces. Nobody better. Blah, blah, blah. *Great interfaces. No wonder he was so busy.*

"Did you get to keep your stock options? When you left the company?" I asked when he paused for a sip of acid.

He smiled at me. "What a question. Any other woman would have asked what she looks like."

"I just wondered how it was handled."

You go, girl, Rational said.

"Yeah, the stocks vested. I even got a severance package. The boss wanted to remain friends, no hard feelings. He was supposed to be happily married at the time and wanted me to be highly motivated to keep the whole mess under wraps. Davis Construction thanks him."

I smiled back. "What does she look like?"

"His wife?"

I just looked at him.

"Okay. Dark hair. White skin. Built. Kind of a sexy Snow White."

Whoa. TMI! Way too much information. I now wished I hadn't asked what Hot Links—my evil little name for the other woman—looked like. I could have done without the sexy Snow White image.

"Where is she tonight? Out of town?" I asked quietly. The rules of engagement stated that I didn't have to be nice since there was another woman in the picture. So I wasn't.

"No. That's just it. We were supposed to meet for dinner but I wanted to be with you tonight. I cancelled and spent the whole night talking to your grumpy father instead."

"Stepfather."

"Yeah."

"Did you eat?" I asked. One of my ironclad rules since high school had been no serious discussions with guys if they're hungry or tired. They get that little frown-wrinkle between their eyes and keep it there regardless of what you say. I needed Brad to be here, fully engaged.

"Dylan, you ask the craziest things. Yes, thank you, I grabbed a bite between phone calls. How about you?"

"So tell me," I said, sitting up straight, hands still in my lap. "Why *did* you want to see me?"

"I was thinking about you last night and I had this, this..." He groped for the word.

"Epiphany?"

He looked at me blankly for a second, the way people do when your help is not helpful. He said, "I was going to say 'thought.' I can't imagine telling someone I had an epiphany. Not with a straight face. But, yeah, let's call it an epiphany, or at least a realization. Here's the deal... Apparently things with my dad and his wife haven't been good lately."

Oh, no. Were we going to have disclosures about Candy Love now, too? A girl could handle only so many revelations in one night.

"What?" he asked.

"I didn't say anything."

"I know but you had a weird look on your face," he pointed out rather ungallantly.

"I thought you were going to tell me something about you and Candy Love."

"Who?"

Oops. That had just slipped out. "Um. Your stepmother." I tried to sound reasonable, wishing I'd kept my face still and my mouth shut. "I'm sorry. You were saying...?"

He mouthed the words *Candy Love.*

"It's nothing." It was clear I was gonna have to explain if I wanted him to go on. And I did. "It's just that I give names to people when I don't know their real names. Probably some leftover vestige from my techie days. You know, you have to name everything when you program. Candy Love is easier for me to think of than Brad's father's wife or Brad's stepmother what's-her-name. It's not a big deal, just something I do." I hoped I wasn't sounding defensive. I sounded kind of defensive to myself.

His grin widened. "Candy Love is perfect. I think I'll start calling her that, too. My stepmother, Candy Love." Then he went still, narrowed his eyes and asked, "What do you call me?"

"Nothing! I mean nothing besides Brad. I know your name so it's not an issue." *The Guy, Manly Man, Magnet Man, Evil Twin, Brad #1*—none of these counted.

He looked unconvinced for a moment. "What did you name the woman I was just telling you about? I don't think I told you her name."

Oh, what I wouldn't have given to have a poker face. "Maybe I didn't have time to name her."

He waited.

"Maybe I don't want to think about her. Maybe I didn't want to give her a name."

"You did. I can tell."

"Maybe you don't want to know." The whole time my brain was cranking, trying to think of another, less inflammatory name.

"Yes, I do," he chuckled, enjoying himself far too much.

"Patty Partner."

"Nah. You'd come up with a better one than that. Candy Love is too perfect. Come on, Sky. Give."

I waited a couple of beats to see if he'd let me off the hook. Nope.

"Miss Inter Face," I lied again.

He looked as if he thought it possible, but then moved his fingers in that come-on-fork-it-over gesture.

"Okay," I relented, but I still didn't tell him.

"Sky Dylan..." He leaned his head forward expectantly.

I chewed on my lower lip.

One of his eyebrows went way up.

That, I couldn't resist. "Hot Links," I said, deadpan.

We both cracked up at the same time. I liked this guy. *Like him, that's all,* I told Rational. *Because he's funny and nice and so, so sexy.*

Rational didn't answer. She wasn't speaking to me.

"Anyway, you were saying, you had this epiphany...?" I prompted. *Us! Let's get back to you and me.*

"Yeah, my epiphany." He suddenly got very serious. And sad. "Well..." He took a deep breath. He did that a lot—take big, ragged breaths. That first night I'd interpreted them as feelings for me. By now I knew that life kept him on the constant verge of hyperventilation and he was just trying to get a little oxygen into his stressed-out lungs. "I've lost Emily, my little sister. She and Candy Love have already moved to California. Candy and my dad are going to get divorced. With them split up, I don't know how much I'll get to see Emily and I love that little kid. She's my sister, my only sister. She calls me bro," he told me again.

"Oh, Brad. I'm so sorry." I was thinking how I'd feel if I lost Asia or Grey. But that was never going to happen. Never. "Maybe you will get to see her," I added doubtfully.

"Nah. It's hard enough to keep it together when everybody likes each other."

"You know what you can do?" I'm a problem solver; I can't not do it. "It's not much consolation, I know, but it's better than nothing. You can make sure you always keep in touch with Emily. Send her Valentine's cards and birthday presents, stuff like that. As she gets older she'll already know you and like you. You'll have chances to see her and that'll make it easier to get reacquainted."

He looked at me, clearly wondering how dense a person could be. "I wanted to watch her grow up. Go to her soccer games. Dance recitals. Not do Hallmark."

"Yeah, I know. I'm so sorry." I hated divorce.

We sat there under the fluorescent lights, not drinking our coffee.

"So, back to my realization," Brad said after a while. "I was thinking about losing Emily and how I hated it and thinking that you were probably the only person I knew who could even begin to understand. And then I thought, what am I doing with someone else?" He said it theatrically, the way Andie does when she forgets she's not at work with her microphone. I half expected an expansive arm gesture to accompany his words. "I'm with someone I don't even really like, much less love. This thing with Hot Links—" he grinned as he said her name "—is all about convenience.

The ex-boss stayed with his wife. Hot Links was at loose ends. I didn't have to burn up precious time." Then he added in his soft voice, "But since I met you, that's not good enough anymore. So I ended it. Last night."

I was quiet for a minute, watching his face, seeing if he meant it. "I need to find a recharge cord for my cell phone," I said. "It's dead."

He gave me one of his I-can't-believe-you-just-said-that looks.

"What?" I asked as innocently as I could.

He didn't move, apparently just waiting for whatever it was I was going to say.

"I don't know *what* to say." I shrugged, uncomfortable.

"Well, tell me what you think," he coaxed.

"I don't know what I think about...anything you just said. And you've said a bunch. I'm still trying to deal with the fact that there *is*—or was—a Hot Links, let alone figure out how I feel about her...and you and her...and me and you. I'm afraid it's going to have to process a while before I have any valid output." *What is wrong with you? Valid output?*

What I really wanted to do was bolt from the table and hit the tollway so fast my Jeep wouldn't even register as I flew by the booth. Things were getting sticky, close, and I needed to breathe. In those personality tests, the ones that put you in one of four boxes, I always came out in the corner that screams: avoid! Bail out and run!

"What kind of phone?" he asked. The boy read signals well, knew to back off. He seemed lighter than he had all evening and I didn't think he was faking. Light and easy. Like he'd lost a few rubber bands himself. Confession is good for the soul.

Not that there had been anything to confess. Not to me. What did I think? That the rescue or those few kisses had made him mine? I could see that night more clearly now, and see why he'd been holding back. He and I certainly didn't have any kind of connection that would lay claim to proprietary rights. If anyone had any rights to him it was Hot Links. I was just Nerd Girl—someone he could talk Internet stuff to and get mild interest from in return.

I felt like throwing up. I did the only thing I could think of—dug my phone out of my purse and showed it to him.

"Hey. I have this exact phone at home. I kid you not, it's *exactly* the same," he said, sounding positively jubilant, turning the phone over in his hand. "I don't use it anymore. I just bought one with a camera. You can *have* the charger."

"Okay...thanks," I said, evenly, not letting myself think about Hot Links or epiphanies or what he'd just said. The "at home" part.

And before I knew it, Wednesday night had become Thursday morning and I was standing in Brad's monastic living room with my skirt hiked halfway up my thighs, my bottom cupped in his strong, hard hands and three of my silk blouse buttons undone.

So much for Rational.

10

LATER, WHEN I RECONSTRUCTED the events in a painful exercise to help explain myself to me, I could clearly recall leaving the Pancake House. I remember thinking how great it was that I wouldn't have to use Step Away's phone early the next morning for my calls. And that was the last clear thought I had as I followed Brad's car to his North Dallas apartment, never for one millisecond allowing myself to speculate on what might happen when we got there.

As soon as we were through his front door, Brad left me and went to look for the cord in his bedroom. I could hear him rummaging around in there while I stood in his nobody-really-lives-here living room. I don't remember studying the room at the time, but I must have given it more than a cursory glance because I could recall it in precise detail when I was doing my mental reenactment.

To say that the apartment was Spartan would be like saying Bill Gates had money. The living room was furnished with five folding tables—the sturdy kind that hotels use for banquets—lined up end-to-end against two adjoining walls to form an *L*. In front of these was one lonesome, ergonomically correct office chair. There were a couple of computers on top of the tables with peripherals of every description hanging off them—a large color printer and a smaller copier-scanner-fax bookended the wired-up snarl.

Aside from a gooseneck lamp, one neatly cascading stack of paper and a single blueprint—held down by a coffee mug, a measuring tape, a book and one of the dress shoes I recognized from number eleven—there was absolutely nothing else in the room. Nothing. Not even lint.

If there were any clues to the inner-Brad in that room I was too focused elsewhere to decipher them. My receivers were locked on the bedroom-Brad. I listened to every little sound he made in his search, seeing him in my mind's eye as he opened drawers and poked around. I tried to predict the exact moment he would reappear. I think I must have been holding my breath.

I watched him as he came back in the room. In slow motion. It took him forever to reach me.

"Here you go," he said, and his voice kind of broke, as he put the cord in my outstretched hand.

We both knew what was going to happen next. There was an inevitability about the tale we'd been spinning since we left the restaurant. Watching my eyes the whole time, his fingers inched up my arm, crept down my back and he pulled my body into his. And then, just like that, time cranked itself up to double speed. The room spun. Our bodies thwacked together and I accidentally boinked the side of his face with the recharge cord as my arms went round his neck, but we didn't stop. Nothing was going to interrupt this tale.

Our bodies remembered. We started at square ten, picked up right where we'd left off three weeks before. His mouth covered mine just like the last time and my lips and tongue answered instantly, knew exactly the way to kiss him back. He ran the fingers of one hand over my breasts, letting his fingernails lightly—ooh, so lightly—scratch the silky layers of cloth over my skin. My nipples rose to catch the soft strokes. His hand began to cuddle my breast, his other hand stroked my back, tracing every curve and mound of my body.

I let myself flow into him, let myself be swept up in the wanting. As his mouth wandered from my lips to my neck, moans gurgled—deep, hungry groans—from inside both of us. He bent to kiss the top of a breast where it popped out over my camisole, then leaned in to drill under the lace of my bra, probing and finding my nipple with the very tip of his tongue. His mouth was full on my breast, then, sucking it, licking it and everything he did, every magic caress of his mouth and his hands, I felt between my legs until it ached there. I needed to feel his whole body against me, have his lips back on my mouth and, sensing it, he straightened to kiss me again.

Right at that moment, when the ache was too great, when I needed this man more than anything in my life, something like Fear chose to creep out of the dark and grab me. She drew the back of her Arctic hand over my forehead, down the side of my cheek and across my neck. And then she started to squeeze, to clamp her frozen fingers around my throat until I panicked.

I managed to squeak out a pitiful, "I've got to go."

"Oh, Sky, baby, no," he said, reaching out for me.

I took an evasive side step and began pulling and tucking my clothes back in order with wild, uncoordinated moves. "Bye," I said, lunging for the door and snatching up my purse where I'd dropped it, making sure no part of my body was within easy grabbing range.

Brad stayed fixed in his spot. I can only imagine what he was thinking; I didn't turn to look at his face as I reached for the knob.

I couldn't get the door open. Of course not. With my purse in one hand and the recharge cord in the other, I pulled and I pushed. I tried moving the locking lever up, then across and nothing worked. I started to cry for the first time in years—not pretty, dainty, little tears like some girls, but great, gulping, rasping, gasps like a drowning ox.

Brad came over, reached around me and opened the door. "Sky? Dylan? Talk to me." He put his hand on my shoulder and I bolted out the door, catching my heel on the threshold and stumbling into the hallway. I was too embarrassed to say anything. Fear and Panic screeched in my head.

I raced down the stairs to my car, pulling out my car keys as I ran, and somehow got the car door unlocked. I jumped in, locked the door, started the Jeep. That's when Misery found me. *My God! Is there anything I can't mess up?*

No, Rational replied. *There's absolutely nothing you can't mess up.*

I couldn't explain my reaction, didn't know where it had come from. My body gave up and collapsed into a heap. Right on top of the steering wheel. *Hooonk.* I shot straight up in the air. That shut me up like a dose of shock therapy. *You are an ass, Sky Dylan Stone,* I thought. My first clear thought since leaving the restaurant.

I saw movement out of the corner of my eye and turned to see Brad running out into the parking lot from the apartment building.

"I'm sorry," I mouthed to him through the windshield as I gunned the Jeep backward out of its parking place. But I doubt he could see my face behind the headlights. *Thump!* The Jeep's rear wheels banged over the short barrier lining the lot. I had to throw it into first gear and floor the pedal to get the wheels back over the hump. Wisely Brad stayed to the side, out of the way, looking scared. Who could blame him? Was there anything more frightening than an out-of-control woman? *Yes, an out-of-control woman in a four-wheel-drive vehicle.*

I sat there a moment, only a few feet back from where I'd started. Brad and I looked at each other through the windshield. He was probably staring at my dark silhouette, but I could see him. Confusion was written all over his face. Misery came sniveling back and I started sobbing again as I turned and drove slowly and cautiously out of the apartment complex maze, making only a dozen or so wrong turns before I was back in familiar territory, heading north on the tollway to Single Town.

Maybe I should have eaten something, after all.

11

IN A PERFECT WORLD there would be no morning after.

Or if there was, it would be filled with beautiful, smiling children who stood guard outside your bedroom door and made sure that you weren't disturbed until you were ready to face the world.

"Sis! Sis!" Asia and Grey screamed as they exploded onto my bed in one of the upstairs guest bedrooms mere seconds, it seemed, after I'd straggled back to Leila's.

I willed away the thought of last night. "What time is it?" I moaned into the pillows without moving a single muscle, not even the one that works my mouth.

"6:07," Grey said. I could imagine him peering at the too-cool-for-words Fossil watch I'd given him. "A.M."

Asia slid off the bed, found my arm with one hand and began gently pulling me toward the edge. "Rise, my child. Rise and be saved," she droned in her husky voice, her face and other arm raised beatifically to the ceiling. "Rise anew and face the coming day." Then, getting impatient with my lack of response, she put both arms into action, tugging with more effect. "C'mon, sis, move your butt," she grunted and heaved. "Have breakfast with us, before we go to school. *Please.*"

Oh, I adored these two and I would deny them nothing, not even the dubious pleasure of my company on this, the morning after my debut as Princess Horse's Ass. *Don't think about it, Dylan!* I squinted my tear-swollen eyes open a crack. They stung like crazy. "Two burnt holes in a blanket," Grandma Frank would've said. I closed them again.

"Sis, get up. It's 6:08," Grey the clock chimed.

I sat up, got my feet down on the floor and moving, washed my wasted face in the bathroom while they banged out a rhythm on the door and the three of us finally tromped down the back stairs.

"6:14," Grey announced.

I could never get enough of these kids. I'd started asking Leila for a baby—or a horse—as soon as I could talk. Her answer was always the same, "Dylan, sweetheart," she'd say. "You can have one when you're old enough to take care of it." She had Asia when I was a capable eleven. My own little baby to love and cuddle, to play with and haul around on my skinny hips, to bathe, to dress and to feed, to wake up with and put to bed. I never asked for any more siblings, though. Or even a horse. I was too pooped.

A reasonable question would be: and just where was the mother while all that bathing, feeding and pooping was going on? But I didn't mind. Those were the stressful years, when Leila was all on her own with five mouths to feed—counting the two dogs—before she gave up on the corporate world. When she was still trying to squeeze her dazzling spirit into a dull-gray box.

Asia was born in New Mexico, Leila's spawning ground. Leila liked living with Texans, but she didn't want any of us to carry around the stigma of being one.

On the time line of Leila Loves, Asia's father, Drew, came right after Two Step. Leila preferred the musical chairs method for selecting her partners. The moment the music stopped, she'd fling herself into the nearest empty lap. Random selection. It made for interesting relationships. At least she opted for empty laps—married guys would have complicated things exponentially.

"Sis," Grey interrupted my reverie. "What does it feel like to read minds?" His little voice was quiet on the stairs behind me.

What did normal families talk about?

Grey had come along four years after Asia. He wasn't premeditated, either. Leila said she'd gotten pregnant on every major birth control method. I think Grey was the leaky-condom baby. It was a new decade and a different era by that time—the tranquil period, the years that began, ironically enough, with Step Away. By the time Leila married him, I'd moved twenty-eight times, gone to nineteen different schools and had endured four different strangers playing daddy to me. Grey had lived his whole life with his biological mother and father, most of it in a seven-bedroom, stone and brick home with nine toilets and a swimming pool. It was as though Leila was running her own sociological study and Grey was the control group.

"Nobody can read minds, stupid," Asia said.

"Mama and Grandma can," he said. "They do it all the time."

"No, little one," I said. "It's not really reading minds. It just seems like it."

"Yeah, well," Grey argued. "Sometimes I think I can, too."

"If I could do that, I'd use it to find people," Asia said.

"Now who's stupid," Grey said to himself.

We'd reached the monster kitchen. All granite and antiqued cherry cabinets. I can't believe it, but I didn't quiz Asia, didn't ask her who she wanted to find. I plopped down at the round table, starving. Breakdowns always did that to me.

"Are there any bagels?" I asked Asia. "Something whole grain?"

She grunted. "Like any other kind would be allowed."

Leila had neglected to outgrow her hippie-holistic ideas about food. She just kept getting more so. Which was okay, since the whole country seemed to be moving right along with her.

"Oh, sis, I forgot," Grey said, sitting down next to me. "You have an e-mail from Brad."

My poor old red eyes sprang out of their sockets, boinked onto the table and popped back into my head. I leaned over until my nose was almost touching his. "Pardon me?"

"An e-mail. From Brad," my little cherub replied. "Your boyfriend." He sang the last word the way you're required to do when you're eight.

Three emotions hit me. First, ecstasy. I wanted to dance and a tiny pilot light of hope ignited within me. But it was quickly extinguished with toe-curling dread. How could I possibly explain myself? I couldn't. How could I face Brad? I couldn't. Then, finally, outrage took over. "Grey! You can't read other people's e-mail!"

"Yes, I can. It's a cinch." He tried to snap his fingers.

"That's not what I mean! It's wrong to read other people's mail. Invasion of privacy. Is this ringing a bell? It's very, very wrong."

He looked down, hurt. It took effort to be upset with Grey, with his long black lashes and chubby cheeks. More effort than I could muster after last night. Outrage was melting into annoyance, and I was rapidly losing my grip on even that.

"It's nunya, Grey," Asia told him then explained to her clueless old sister. "None of your business."

"Yeah, that's right," I agreed. "Nunya." But the geeky part of my brain couldn't resist asking, "How'd you get in?"

"I'm a hackler," he said, looking up, smiling again.

"You mean a hacker."

"No. Hackler. It's a hacker who doesn't do bad stuff. Like

a heckler." He beamed a smile full of missing teeth at me. "I made that up."

"He just watches people," Asia, the explainer, told me. "When they type their passwords, he can tell what keys they press by the position of their fingers. If your index finger is like this, it's an *F*. If it's like this, it's an *R* or like this, it's a *T*," she said, moving her finger in a little triangle to demonstrate. "He's gotten really good at it. He probably watched you when you were here last time."

"Why don't you just read their thoughts?" I teased.

"Wait a minute! So it's okay to read minds but not e-mails?" he asked. "I'm not sure I get all this."

"What did he say?" We all looked over at Leila as she wandered into the kitchen wearing a long batik bathrobe—the greens and purples setting off the red of her hair and her tight, white legs peeking out of the slit.

She always looks beautiful, I thought, *even in the morning. No wonder the men all love her.*

"Hackler," Asia said.

"No, I mean Brad. What did the e-mail say?" Leila asked.

"Leila!" I cried, indignant all over again. "It's wrong!"

Grey gave me a dirty look and mouthed "Mama" at me. He hated it that I didn't call her that. But "mama" hadn't really expressed Leila's personality back in the reckless years. I mouthed a "Sorry" back at him.

Leila came over and stood behind Grey and put her cheek down to his so he couldn't see the laughter in her eyes. "Dylan's right, little guy. No more, okay?"

He nodded solemnly and she pecked his cheek—which is all he would allow nowadays—before sliding into a chair across from me, the look of motherhood-well-done on her face.

"You've got to admit, though," she said, the techie in her showing up, "it's some talent."

"What *did* it say?" Asia asked. The whole family—except, of course, Step Away, who wasn't family—took an active interest in my love life and the miserable lack thereof. There's something about an eligible girl being unattached that makes people uncomfortable. My family needed me to have someone in my life, even more than I did. Okay, not really. I just said that to make a point.

Grey was looking to me, waiting for permission.

"It's okay, buddy. This time." I wasn't worried. Brad had perfected an impersonal e-mail style. "But no more snooping, okay?" Note to self: *change password*.

Grey flashed us a cereal-laden smile. "Call," he said.

"That's it?" Asia and Leila chorused.

He nodded. "Except for an exclamation mark at the end."

"Brad's pretty busy..." I began.

"Ya think?" Asia said, clearly disappointed. She wanted *Cinderella* and I was giving her *Mating Rites of Computer Nerds*.

Leila stood up. Her gaze danced over my face for several seconds. "What's he like, Dylan?"

"A soul mate," I said, while Rational yelled all kinds of objections in my head. I ignored her.

"So what's the problem?" she asked.

"Me."

She smiled at me, her liquid, Dylan-I-love-you smile. "You need to find a way to make yourself happy."

"I'm happy," I said and batted my bloodshot eyes at her.

She shook her head. "Coffee?" she asked, holding up my favorite mug, the one with the hand-painted sunflowers. I nodded.

Okay, now I *was* happy. On any morning, but especially on a morning after, happiness was having someone bring you coffee just the way you like it. In your favorite mug.

Sitting there in Leila's elegant faux-painted breakfast

room, I tried to decide what to do about last night. I summoned Rational to help me but she was too embarrassed.

What had I been thinking? Why didn't I just tell him I was a virgin?

12

SOMETIMES, IT'S OKAY to be a virgin.

Like when you're fifteen or seventeen or hell, even twenty.

I can think of half a dozen other situations when it's not only okay, it's a damn good idea.

Like if you have AIDS.

Or your elegantly bearded son is going to start a major new religion based on the fact.

Or you're a young pop star with an adorable face and a fantastic belly button and you make a ton of money advertising your maidenhead.

Or you have no choice. Because your nutzo, zealot male relatives have gotten their masculinity all mixed up with your virginity and they'll torture or maybe kill you for shaming them if you even think of dropping your veil.

Or you're the heroine of a romance novel and you lose it on page eighty-six to the guy with the big pecs and long hair on the cover.

Or you're super-religious and want to wait till you're married.

But lots of times it's *not* okay. Like when life got messy early and things just hadn't worked out like you planned. Your friends were settling down and you hadn't even gotten started yet. Then it was just plain mortifying.

I'm not even sure when things changed, when I quit fighting off the guys who pretended they wanted nothing more out of life than to sleep with me. All I know is, by the time I was a senior in college, it had gone from being a prize to a problem and I couldn't have paid someone to do the deed.

Back then if I had a problem, Andie and Eva had a problem, so they tackled it for me.

"Maybe we could auction it off. Go for the highest bidder," Andie suggested one night. Good thing we were still in college and she wasn't a voice talent yet. She'd have wanted to use a microphone. "Ladies and gentlemen, I'd like to direct your attention to center stage. This beauty is packing a..."

She started getting into her plan, developing it. "Remember the chick in *Memoirs of a Geisha*? They sold it to the highest bidder! I'll bet there's still a market for maidenheads out there in some little repressed corner of the world."

I could feel her looking at me. I glanced up. Good Lord, she was serious. I went back to my homework.

"How bad could it be?" she asked. "One night. Fifty grand."

"Why only fifty?" Eva asked, suspicious of any bargain.

"You're right," Andie agreed. "What am I thinking? A hundred grand, easy."

"I don't know. That might be high." I could feel Eva's stare, looking me up and down.

"You think they'd pay extra for the boobs...?" she asked doubtfully.

"Ladies, please," I said.

"Dylan's worth it," Andie defended me...or maybe my boobs. "Anyway, people will pay for anything. Top dollar if it's marketed right." As if she had a clue what she was talking about.

I glanced up to see what Eva, Toppo-Supreme, thought about Andie's economic theories. She was nodding. Eva knew a lot about paying top dollar.

"Dylan? Who do we know in marketing?" Andie asked.

Somebody stop them.

"Chris!" Andie hollered, answering her own question. "Chris what's his name? The guy with the baggy shorts and those shirts. I'm pretty sure he's marketing. Or is it finance?"

"You're not talking about the flip-flops guy?" Eva asked.

"Yeah. Maybe we could ask him."

"What? If he'd sleep with her?" Eva asked, not sounding nearly as indignant as I felt.

"Pay attention! We're talking marketing here," Andie cried.

"You know, though...he's not really all that bad," Eva said. "Not really. Except his feet are always dirty. But he can't have had that many girlfriends. He might be desperate. I bet he'd do it if the three of us asked him. All together. And Dylan promised there wouldn't be any repercussions. You know...she wouldn't freak out or fall in love or anything."

It was then that I'd decided I'd better do something about it. Myself. Without their help. I could see that I'd been waiting too long for Mr. Flawless. From then on, I was going to settle for Mr. Not-Too-Bad-All-Things-Considered.

I needed a plan, an approach. So the first thing I tried was honesty. It's what I'd been weaned on: Be yourself, Dylan. Truth is beautiful. Real is right.

It's pretty obvious how that plan worked, since I was still agonizing over the whole stupid thing three years later. Roger was my first test case.

We were in his bedroom, in his bed, tossing around in his semi-yucky, rarely laundered sheets. We'd met because we had the same major—the really nasty, technical one that I don't like to bring up since it conjures all those stringy-haired, earnest and intense stereotypes. Things had just sort

of happened between us because we had so many classes together. We started out talking on breaks between classes,
then moved on to grabbing a quick beer afterward. We were
perfect for each other. Roger was the only guy in those techie classes with clean hair and no sign of the ubiquitous
tummy slump and I was the only female. Plus we both had
a flair for extraneous detail. It was a match made in a base-
ment computer lab.

He had eventually gotten around to inviting me to some
major frat party, something like the annual Sigma Chi
Sigma De-flowering Fête. One of those deals where they got
pledges to chauffeur you around so you could get ham-
mered slugging down shots in the back seat while your date
tried to have sex with you. By this time Roger and I had
been going out for a while and had come to the point—that
critical dating crossroads where you either get intimate or
get out. He knew it, I knew it and, after a few turns around
the block looking for Roger's apartment, so did the designated driver.

It was time. I was ready.

It went something like this: Kiss, kiss, squeeze, squeeze.

"Roger there's something I have to tell you."

"Don't worry about it, baby." Pant, pant. "I have some in
the drawer." Stretch, reach.

"No, not that. Um. Something else."

The arm he'd been reaching with fell to the floor. His face
dropped onto the grungy sheets. "Oh, damn. You don't
have your period do you? Shit! You should have said something before."

I was quiet a minute trying to imagine that conversation
in my head.

"Hey, Dylan. Next Saturday, you wanna go to a party?"

"I can't."

"Why not?"

"Because I'll be...I'm—"

"You'll be what?"

"I..."

"What?"

I should have been born a couple of centuries earlier.

"Roger, I'm a virgin," I said finally, delivering one of the best lines. Ever.

Roger didn't think so. I could have whipped those nasty sheets off the bed and thrown him off the balcony wrapped up inside and I would have gotten a more favorable response.

"What do you mean?" he asked, flipping onto his back, staring up at the ceiling.

"I don't know how else to say it."

He was up on one elbow. "You mean like virgin, virgin?" He was smart, really, I promise you. It was the unexpectedness of it all, I'm sure.

"Yeah."

Maybe he said something else, and maybe I did, too, but within seconds he was gone. It was *his* apartment! I put on the pieces of clothing that I'd had so much help shedding and walked the three miles to my apartment. I waited with Honesty to hear from him. And waited, and waited. I think he must have changed majors. It was probably for the better. He wasn't all *that* good at details.

The next time was with this guy I happened to meet when he was performing at Austin's annual music festival, South-by-Southwest. He was the son of somebody famous. Or at least the father's band was famous and had been since the Stone Age. This guy, the son, had been around, was getting pretty well known himself and his reputation had preceded him into town—Major Hunk. It was perfect. He'd be out of Austin by the time the festival was over. Ten days, max. I figured he wouldn't have to worry about me getting all mushy and likewise. Miscalculation number two million, seventy-four.

It started out well enough. We met, fooled around a little, saw each other for the next few days. The fourth night, he took me to watch his band and afterward we hit the hot spots around Sixth Street. We got to his hotel about three in the morning. It was a perfect setting and this time, I was more than ready. The sheets were clean, I was wearing my new black French underwear—or at least the three strings that made up the bottom half—and my head was clear. I didn't drink much at the bars because I'd been in training.

This was it.

Everything was wonderful. *He* was wonderful—hot, cool, sexy and aloof. All we needed was Leila's Dylan tapes playing in the background.

This time my approach would be different. Forget Honesty. I wasn't going to tell him. I'd just go with the flow. Take it as it came. Be cool.

And it was so flowing. And I was so cool. A condom appeared and the three strings vanished. But then we got down to the taking it as it comes part and I'd forgotten to take into consideration size—my size, his size and their dimensions relative to one another. Miscalculation two million, seventy-five. Except it wasn't exactly a miscalculation. I hadn't even thought about it.

"What's the deal?" he said, rolling off me sideways.

"I guess I haven't done this before." Okay, forget cool.

"What? Like never?" He was up on one elbow. "Like...*virgin*?" I wondered if guys always had to ask that while they were propped up on an elbow.

"Yeah." I got up on my elbow, too.

"Oh, man."

Kiss, kiss. "No, really, it's okay. I'm ready for this. You don't have to worry. Honest. I *want* to do this."

"How old are you?"

"Twenty-one."

"And you're a fricking virgin?" He sat up.

"It was kind of an accident." I sat up, too. I was getting desperate so I didn't cover myself with the sheets.

"Oh, man. I can't do this." He didn't look at me. He plucked off the condom, jumped out of bed and started looking around the room for his clothes.

"If you're worried that I'm saving myself for marriage, I'm not. I know that freaks guys out. But I'm not. Really."

"Yeah. But you can't do it like this. With me."

"Yes, I can. You're just right. You do this a lot."

He thought about that a minute. "Well, not with virgins. Not with, you know, real girls."

I saw one of those blow-up rubber dolls in my head.

"I mean...nice girls."

"I'm not nice. I want this. Please, come back to bed."

Naked + begging = new low.

"Man, you've waited this long, it's gotta be good. It's gotta mean something." He'd found his underwear and shirt and was putting them on.

"No, it doesn't. It doesn't have to mean anything."

"Yeah. It does. Don't talk like that. I'd hate me. You'd hate me. For the rest of your life. I gotta go."

"It's your hotel room."

"Yeah. Well. I'll see you around. I'm sorry, all right? I really am." He took his key and right before he left, he turned and looked at me sitting on the bed. "You are so perfect," he said. The door closed. Yeah, I felt perfect, all right. I sat there a minute, trying to switch gears, to get up the energy to search for my clothing in the covers and on the floor and way over there by the desk. I could see the condom hanging like molted skin on the lip of the trash can. The door opened a crack.

"They'll get you a cab downstairs when you're ready. I'll take care of everything so don't pay him again. Okay?" The door closed. The door opened. "Good luck," he said and this time the door stayed closed.

No more miscalculations, Rational said. *The next time you plan to seduce somebody, how about making sure you bring the damn car.* Rational was getting testy.

The next time was in New Mexico and I didn't need a car. I went there for Spring Break with French, one of my buddies and a fellow New Mexican. We were good friends. Not like Eva and Andie—there are some things you just can't tell a guy—but still, we were tight. It was my senior year and his final year of law school and all I can say is, it had seemed like a good idea at the time.

French and I had decided to go to New Mexico for the break because the rest of the world was going the other way, bound for sand and sea. New Mexicans just love being different. We got excited talking about it. We could go here, we could go there, I'll show you this, you can show me that. We flew into Albuquerque, rented a camping van and headed north toward Santa Fe. Into hundred mile an hour winds. A Sahara sandstorm with tumbleweeds. Oh, how quickly we forget. Spring in New Mexico isn't.

Within minutes, every molecule of moisture was sucked from our bodies. Lips chapped, hair stood on end, fingers miraculously grew hangnails and our skin crackled into alligator hide which, after a couple more days, started to flake off like dandruff. We hunkered down in our little camper, shivering and shaking in the wind and waited it out. We played cards, ate Mexican food, drank Coronas. It was great to be home.

The third night, Silence woke us up. The wind had died and there were delicate hints of chamisa and sage and piñon trees in the lingering breeze. We hauled our sleeping bags out into the night and lay there, bundled up against the cold desert air, singing hokey old cowboy songs, laughing and communing with the stars. The Land of Enchantment had delivered on its promise.

After a while, French rolled over on his side in his sleeping bag, propped himself up on one elbow and looked at me. "Dylan?" he began.

"Mmm-hmm."

"Tell me something."

"Okay."

"Are you a...um...a..."

"Yeah," I said. "Why?" I tried to act as if it was no big deal. I stayed on my back, looking up at the sky and waited. Totally low-key. But I'd spent the past three days in that vibrating metal can getting hooked on this guy. Feeling so incredibly close to him, realizing how great he was and thinking we should be together. So really, this was a big deal.

"I don't know. Someone told me. I didn't believe them."

"Well, believe it."

"Wow. I didn't think that was possible."

I sighed.

"You should have told me," he said in a voice I hadn't heard before. Low and sexy. My goose bumps went double-decker.

"You don't mind?" I whispered, still lying on my back, afraid to get my hopes up.

"No. You crazy? Not at all," he said and reached into my sleeping bag to touch my arm.

"Promise?" I turned on my side to face him and tucked one arm beneath my head.

"In fact," he said as he began to rub my shoulder, "I think it's kind of sexy."

If I could have painted my dreams into a picture it would

have been just like that night, with those scents and sounds around me. I closed my eyes and waited for him to kiss me.

"You know, I have a friend…"

Eyes opened.

"I think you'd really like her," he said, running his fingers down my arm. "Maybe the three of us…"

I started to say something, but only this strangled little noise came out, as if an entire hamburger was caught in my throat.

"Or if not," he said, rubbing faster, all eager to please, "I could watch. You know, not really participate. Or anything."

"What are you talking about?" I managed to choke out. He looked as though I'd slapped him. What had I missed? I rewound the conversation in my head.

Ah, said Rational. *He thinks you're a lesbian. Remember, you didn't let him finish. It's always best to let them finish their sentences.*

Oh, shut up, I told her.

Trying to get it straightened out, what everybody meant, and hadn't meant, we got so embarrassed we just went to sleep to avoid the whole damn mess. We woke up at dawn, two solid blocks of ice—nights are cold in the desert—and tried again to sort things out, to go back in time—something that was never going to happen. Through all the "I thoughts" and the "I didn't means," one fact remained enormously clear: he wasn't interested. Not one bit. Not in me, by myself. And most especially not if I was a virgin.

"But, Dylan, can't we still be friends?"

I thought only girls said that.

By breakfast time we just gave up and ate our huevos rancheros. There was nothing more to say.

That afternoon while we were checking out the rugs in Chimayo and not talking some more, we ran into an acquaintance of French's from Austin—a friend of a friend of somebody's sister. French flung himself into her arms—really. At first Melissa was a little surprised, taken aback by his exuberance, but she rallied quickly and was soon returning his enthusiasm, exclamation mark for exclamation mark.

After the briefest introduction in history, I had plenty of time to observe them. I gathered that she and her parents were roughing it somewhere in the Arctic circle or, at the very least, the most isolated, depressing spot on the planet. No, sorry, I got that wrong. It was that swanky tennis ranch up in Taos. Poor Melissa. So, so alone.

Well, no wonder. She could have had a giant tourist sticker stuck on her forehead. She was wearing a jean jacket, a crisp new embroidered Mexican peasant dress and a turquoise squash blossom necklace made for an extralarge Navajo. Peaking out from a pair of pristine Birkenstocks were ten little toenails painted a brilliant Dallas Red. *These poor Texas girls,* I thought from the vantage point of my old jeans, worn leather jacket and dusty boots. *They just don't get it.*

Well, maybe not. But she got him. I took the van and went down to see Grandma Frank as French left with poor, lonely Melissa in her Range Rover to go to Taos.

It was late evening by the time I got down to Socorro. Grandma Frank met me at the door of her little adobe hacienda, naked. Really, she wasn't all that bad or maybe I'd gotten used to it. I just hoped they discovered some fabulous fix for the boobs and the knees by the time I got to be that old because they were the worst.

"Wait," she said, closing the door. She reappeared in a couple of seconds with one of her hand-loomed shawls held loosely in front of her.

"I thought you'd know I was coming," I said as I leaned

way over to kiss her. Grandma Frank was convinced she was psychic.

"I did," she said, smiling.

So why didn't she get dressed, Rational asked.

Maybe she didn't feel like it, I snapped.

"Come in, sit, get warm, it's cold for April," she said over her shoulder as she and her bony bottom disappeared around a curved wall to her bedroom. I was alone in my favorite place in the world. The womb room. A piñon fire crackled away in the kiva fireplace and roasted green chile smells drifted in from the kitchen. Her loom stood in the only square corner of the room, a long rectangular shawl in deep greens half-finished on its warps. On the brick floor in front of the fireplace laid a huge old Navajo rug, its insect and plant colors still vivid. I squirmed out of my jacket and boots, skated across the smooth red bricks in my socks and hurled myself over the back of a squishy couch, the one facing the fireplace.

I looked around me. At the zigzag latillas in the ceiling, at the oil paintings in the warm ochre tones of enchanted earth, at Grandma Frank's curly-wool shawls brightening the room with the purples and blues of their hand-dyed yarn. Somewhere on the other side of those thick walls stood the twenty-seven satellite dishes that made up the VLA—Very Large Array—the world's largest antennae. *That's why she thinks she's psychic,* I thought. *She's picking up signals.* Except that didn't explain why my mom thought she had telepathic powers, too.

Grandma Frank slipped back into the room, barefoot. I snuck a peek and saw she was all decked out in jeans and a green velvet Navajo shirt with silver buttons. Her short white hair was brushed straight back from her face and her emerald eyes were lit by the flattering color. She looked twenty years younger.

"So, my little one," she said, kissing me on the forehead. "How's life?" She sat with a plop in a low chair.

I sighed and put a pillow over my face.

"Your father called this morning."

"Why?" I sat up. I didn't hear from my dad much. I liked him. A lot. But he had a new woman every five or six years. Some he married, some he didn't. It kept him pretty busy.

"He wanted to know where you were. Wanted me to find you."

"What'd you tell him?"

"I told him I could feel you. That you'd be here soon."

"And?"

"He and Lucy have split up. I think he's lonesome."

I lay back down and put the pillow over my face again. I let out another big sigh. Wow. He was finally rid of the liposuction queen, old Lipo-Lucy. *Does this make me look fat?* "Am I fat?" "Do I look fat to you?" "What's this? Is this FAT?"

As glad as I was to be rid of old Lipo, I knew not to celebrate. A worse one would show up in a couple of months. The women in my dad's life were like those monsters who when you cut off their heads, grew a bigger, slimier, scarier one right away.

"It's never easy," she said.

"What?" I asked after a long pause. I was lost in my own thoughts, trying to imagine a new stepmother worse than Lucy.

"Loving."

"I wouldn't know." But I was toying with a new plan for the virgin thing. I'd wait until I was old and rich and then pay somebody. They'd *have* to pretend to like it.

She didn't say anything for a minute. "Such a lonely pastime," she said, finally.

"What is, love?"

"No, feeling sorry for yourself," she said softly.

"Was that green chile I smelled?" I said. It came out muffled—the pillow was beginning to conform to my face.

"It might be. And some fresh tortillas, I think. Thick the way you like them."

I came out from under the pillow. I could feel the flush in my face. And as I sat up, tears that had been trapped inside all day—or maybe all year—tried to sneak out. But I was too quick for them. I opened my eyes wide and blinked. I looked over at her, watching me as if her soft, green eyes could see inside me, could count each of the little blue rubber bands pinching my heart.

"I'm never going to find anybody, am I, Grandma Frank?"

She tilted her head a little and stared out the window. Maybe she was looking to the VLA to get a reading. Then she smiled the saddest smile I've ever seen.

"No, my child. You won't." She held out her hands for me to help her out of the low seat. "I'm afraid," she said, as I stood there in front of her, tears stinging the back of my eyes, "with all that noise banging around inside you—" she got to her feet then took my face in both of her hands and held me so that she could look right into my eyes "—I'm afraid, my little mess," she said, "that he's going to have to find you."

I swallowed in a gulp. "Really?"

She grinned at me and nodded and I took a deep breath.

We put our arms around each other and followed the wonderful scents to the kitchen. Maybe things weren't really so bad. Back then I was still only twenty-one, not even out of school yet.

There were worse things, I knew, than staying a virgin. Like not having a grandma.

Or green chile stew.

Or thick homemade tortillas.

And I was starving.

13

"WHAT'S GOING ON in here?" Step Away yelled as he came play-roaring into the family room across from the breakfast table. I was thrown from the cozy contemplation of my virgin woes and hurled to that other space. The outsider. Suddenly superfluous.

"Daddy!" Grey jumped up to catch him. But Step Away executed a neat little fake and side step and scooted into the kitchen behind Leila, winding his arms around her waist, kissing the neck exposed by her piled-up hair. "Morning." He nuzzled in her ear. She put down the coffee cup she'd just poured—mine!—and turned to kiss him. They were always like that. We were used to it—or at least the kids were. It gave me the creeps.

Grey, undeterred, ran into the kitchen and wrapped his arms around them both, struggling to encompass all four legs. Leila and Grant broke off their kiss, laughing. They each reached an arm down to include him in their embrace, their hands barely touching on his back. They gave each other secret smiles.

Look at him, said Rational. *He's a loving husband, a great daddy. Did you ever think that maybe step hell is your fault?*

Yeah, I told her, watching them. *Just about all the time.*

Grey was the first to pull away, after a big, noisy squeeze, and zipped back to his breakfast and all three pages of comics in the *Dallas Morning News.*

Asia had raised her eyes from the fashion section to watch

them. And I could feel the sadness gathering around her. *Had Step Away started freezing her out, too?* She felt me staring at her and glanced over for just a moment, lifting the corners of her mouth, trying to tell me she was okay.

Leila handed Step Away the full coffee cup—mine...in the sunflower mug.

"Asia," he said and tipped his head at her. I thought I felt a puff of wintry chill, but I wasn't sure if it was for her or me. I was rewarded with the usual curt head nod and mumbled "Dylan," as he sat down at the breakfast table opposite me.

"Morning." Now the icy winds blew in earnest. Frost began to form on the window, icicles dangled from the overhead light.

There were only four chairs at the table. Perfect for a family of four, which is what they were. I got up to leave with my half-eaten bagel just as the phone rang.

I could feel Step Away's stare on my back. He probably couldn't believe that I answered his phone, but I was sure it was for me.

"Would you come over to Ron's house? Before the luncheon? Oh, no, never mind... Ron says right now."

"Hi, Eva," I said.

"Will you?" she asked again.

"I'm busy," I said. I was planning to hide under a pillow all morning and not think about Brad and last night.

"He wants to talk to you about seating."

"Eva, it's a shower. Not a power-lunch."

"Could you do it?" she purred at me as if I was a guy. "For me?"

"That voice doesn't work on me, Eva. Tell him he can rearrange it any way he wants. I don't care. I don't even know who these people are."

"They're powerful people," she kept cooing.

"So let him seat them where he wants."

"Yeah, that's what he wants to do. He's making up a list for you. Just a few notes. So you won't forget."

I didn't answer. Apparently she didn't require it.

"Ron's house is right here by the club, you know, ten seconds away. Couldn't you just come get the list now so you could be at the club early? Make sure everything's perfect? I'd do it myself but I'm going to the spa as soon as I get off the phone." I could hear the sunshine in her voice. There was nothing in the world Eva liked better than a full morning of pampering. Unless it was a full week of pampering. "I'll just barely get to the club in time as it is."

"Okay," I said, with a sigh. "Have him e-mail it to me." *All you have to do,* I told myself, *is get through the next seventy-something hours, let Eva have her fantasy wedding. Do it for her.* Would this be my life from now on? Helping other people with their lives, making sure everything went smoothly. That's what people did who didn't have a life of their own.

She paused. "Ron doesn't like to do e-mail himself. He's here, not at the office so there's no one to do it for him...."

Silence gave her a minute to ponder just how far she thought she could push me.

"Oh, okay," she said in her dreamy voice. She'd started thinking about something else—probably the Moor mud wrap or the aromatherapy facial at the spa. "See ya."

There was a pillow somewhere calling my name and I intended to go get under it. But first, coffee. I went to get some and the phone started to ring. My heart did a cartwheel. Leila and I locked eyes over the granite bar. Neither of us moved. It rang again. Grey tore over to answer it.

"And whom may I say is calling," Grey asked into the phone, giggling so hard he almost couldn't get the words out. "It's for you," he sang, swinging the cordless phone over his head.

I gave a little wave to all the nice folks staring at me. I could feel Step Away's stink-eye on my back as I slunk away with his phone.

"Hey," I said when I reached the top of the stairs.

"Hey," Brad said.

Silence. We listened to each other breathe.

"I thought I'd go ahead and call," he said finally. "See how you were. If you made it."

"Yeah, yeah I did."

More breathing.

"Are you okay?"

"Yeah." Long pause. "Yeah."

"Are you going to talk to me?" he asked.

"I think I'm too embarrassed," I mumbled, sitting down on the top stair.

"What happened?"

"I kind of freaked out."

"Yeah, Sky. I noticed that. I was asking why."

And that's when the argument started.

Tell him!

I can't.

He's waiting!

What do I say?

Just tell him.

Guys hate it. It's too weird. If I tell him, he's the one who will freak out.

Well, for heaven's sake, say something!

So I started babbling. "I think—and this is just a theory, okay, because I'm not sure—but I think it was because things started moving so fast and I don't really know you that well. I mean *that* well, and I don't know exactly how I feel about everything, all that stuff about Hot Links and all, and instead of calmly relating that fact to you—which, of course, is what I should have done—I sort of panicked.

Probably because I was already kind of in an excited state anyway."

Brad didn't say anything.

"I'm sorry. I don't usually do stuff like that," I said softly.

"I couldn't quit thinking about it." He sounded so serious.

"Which part?" I asked, trying to lighten it up. "The blubbering or the Jeep?"

"The part about you being so scared." So much for light.

"It's just that..." I took a big breath. "I'm really sorry," I said again. There was nothing else to say.

"Okay. So now what?" His voice sounded a little more normal, not so...freaked.

"Yeah, now what?" I figured he'd better make that call. If I were him, I'd run like hell.

"How about today?" he asked.

"Today?" I asked faintly.

Mayday! Mayday! Rational yelled in my head. *Engage gray matter!*

"Yeah. What if I came with you?"

"Today?" *Stop saying that!*

"Why are you so surprised? I freed up my calendar so I could be with you. So...I want to be with you."

"You'd do that?"

"Well, it's lunch and dinner, right? How bad could it be?"

Dr. Sphincter's big shots from the club? Eva's snobby relatives? Bad, real bad.

"There are going to be guys there, right? At the shower?"

"Yeah, at least half. It's mostly for the groom's friends. So Ron can show Eva off."

"Well, what do you think? Can I come with you?"

This is not a good idea, Rational opined.

"Yes. Yes. Please," I said and I'm sure he could feel the

heat blazing through the phone. "Meet me down there at noon?"

"Okay. Good. I can get some work done." He paused then. "It's not going to be as bad as you're making it sound. Right?"

"Oh, no!" I laughed. *Probably much, much worse.*

I sat there wondering what could make him want to do that. Why would he go somewhere he didn't want to and with a confirmed maniac? I grinned as every part of my body got tingly or felt really warm.

The kids came up the stairs to get ready for school. They both leaned down and kissed the top of my head as they passed.

My happy thoughts were interrupted by my freshly charged cell phone. I ran to the bedroom to answer it. It was one of my hottest sales prospects, which meant I should really take the call despite the fact that I technically wasn't working. As soon as I answered, he started yelling, completely freaking out about the political realities in the nether regions of his company and how the guy who was aiming for his own position was going to have a competing company do a sales pitch after mine next week.

I so didn't need to deal with a stressed-out, paranoid executive while Dr. Sphincter impatiently waited for me to sell my soul to ensure his wedding was nothing short of perfect and Step Away lurked nearby to send me yet another deep freeze message. As I listened to my potential client rant, I really just wanted to get some more sleep so that I could enjoy being with Brad. Too bad the sleep thing wasn't going to happen any time soon.

I managed to squeeze in a few words of reassurance, reminding him of the agreements we had and the impressive presentation we'd be doing. "Bob?" I liked the tone I was

projecting—soothing, reasonable. It helped that afte_
night I had no freak-out left.

Despite the words and the tone, he started hollering
earnest. Hollering is far more common in the corporat_
world than you'd imagine. Just as I launched into a list of all
that my company could do, Step Away came into the bedroom with his hand out. I stared at him not knowing what
he wanted.

Step Away stomped over to the desk to pick up his phone
where I'd dropped it. Could the man possibly be more anal?
He stomped out of the room with a final icy glare thrown
my way.

Obviously some of my reassurances hit home because the
hot-under-the-collar prospect finally calmed enough to ex-
tract a promise from me to bring "the big guns" to Tuesday's meeting. I clicked off feeling more exhausted than I
had when Grey and Asia woke me up.

"It's 7:23," the Grey clock chimed as he ran past my room.
He didn't stop to kiss me this time, just waved as he zoomed
by. "Hurry up, Asia! You're gonna miss the bus!"

"Grey!" I said. "Slow down. You've got twelve minutes.
It doesn't take thirty seconds to get to the bus stop."

Asia came in the room and sat on my bed. She rolled her
eyes in the direction Grey had taken. I sat down next to her
and she leaned her head on my shoulder.

"No!" he shouted from the bottom of the stairs, getting
his stuff together. "It might come early. *Eleven minutes.*" The
door slammed behind him. It must be a guy thing.

"I love you, sis," Asia said, forgetting to be cool.

I kissed the top of her head. "I love you, too," I said.

I walked her to the stairs and she clomped down them,
dragging her heavy backpack behind her. *Clomp, thump,
clomp, thump.* What did she have in that thing? At the bottom she turned and blew me a big kiss. I hadn't noticed be-

...looked. Standing there, she could have ...or even older. Had she worn makeup that ... I started missing her and Grey already. I needed ...ck my wedding schedule spreadsheet to see when I'd ...ave some time with them again.

My cell phone rang. What was up with this? It wasn't even eight in the morning! It was Dr. Sphincter. Probably wanting me to come get his stupid list. I sat back down on the bed and didn't answer it.

When it stopped ringing, I called the country club and increased the luncheon count by one. We'd allowed for a few last-minute undecideds, so I didn't really need to bother, but my brain liked accurate counts. Then I called my office and rounded up a couple of token big shots for my Tuesday meeting. They weren't the top dogs but they'd have to do. After that, I called Andie and arranged a time to pick her up.

Now, the important stuff. What to wear from the limited selection I had with me? I needed an outfit that would undo the trauma from last night, put Brad's mind to rest, get rid of any remaining doubts. Something that screamed classy and sane.

My phone rang another time. It was Brad.

I couldn't answer it. I knew he was calling to tell me that something had come up and he couldn't make it, or that he'd reconsidered, he couldn't build a stable relationship with an unstable partner or...whatever. It would be easier if he dumped me on a message. Not in real life. I waited for the message beep, but it didn't sound. I wished I'd answered. Sometimes being an avoider was a drag.

14

I'LL SAY THIS about Eva's ninety-ninth wedding shower—all right, all right, it was only her seventh: I had no idea how much head wounds bleed.

I was on my way down to the luncheon, feeling edgy. I was still obsessing about not answering Brad's call.

I'd opted for a simple, beige linen dress. It fairly shrieked sanity and class. And beige is perfect for country clubs, especially if you throw on lots of heavy gold jewelry. Which I didn't have. Oh, well, no one was going to mistake me for a member anyway.

I zipped off the tollway to pick up Andie. It took her forever to come out, but when she did—finally!—I saw she'd foregone country-club-beige and opted for red. A deep, rich, dark red. Bloodred. And she looked beautiful.

"Did Brad get you last night?" she asked as soon as she'd hauled herself up into my Jeep and gave me the customary dirty look. Jeeps weren't exactly Andie's style.

Get me? Then I remembered he'd called her to get my number.

"He seems nice. Except he doesn't have much money, does he? I can always tell. But, mmm-mmm, that body! What did he want?"

I started to tell her just the safe parts but there weren't many of those so I ended up telling her all about it. The night of virgin madness followed by a second chance.

"Let me get this right," Andie said. "This guy wants to

talk, likes to listen and remembers everything you tell him?"

I nodded with a big old grin spreading across my face.

"He's gay right?"

"Noo."

"Are you sure?"

I gave her my look.

"Okay, except for no money, what's wrong with him?"

Other than being too busy to breathe and, oh yeah, Hot Links... "Nothing."

"Then...?"

"Then what?" I asked her.

"Then why didn't you sleep with the guy?" Andie asked, staring at me. "You are really messed up."

"I don't know. I wanted to. I just kind of freaked out."

"Freaks me out just thinking about it," Andie said, and did a little shiver thing with her shoulders. "I can't believe he called you after all that. I wouldn't have."

And then I had one of my midchat epiphanies. "I'm going to do it," I declared, slapping the steering wheel. "Tonight!"

"Oh, yeah? And what are you going to do about the whole virgin thing? You gonna tell him first?"

"No. Maybe he won't notice."

Andie rolled her eyes. Then a smile opened up her face. "Which reminds me," she said. "I have to tell you something."

"I don't want to talk about it." I was trying to keep my attention on the road. Everybody sped on the tollway. You had to. They'd set the speed limit way too low, trying to shave a life or two off the mortality rate and make up for the staggering death toll on the Central Expressway.

"It's not about *your* virgin mess. Somebody else's."

"Good. I can already tell I don't want to hear it," I said. "We have to be careful with me, I'm fragile right now."

But curiosity got the best of me.

"It's nothing about Brad?" I asked. "Right?"

"Nope."

"Because I'd want to hear it if it was."

Silence.

"Okay, what?" I asked after a while.

"I thought you didn't want to hear it."

I gave her another look. A short one. Traffic was bad.

"Matt and Eva," she said, looking out her window.

"What about them? Zero virgins in that horny group."

"True," she agreed. "But if you add in Ron..."

"Andie, you're killing me. Are you going to tell me?"

"Maybe," she said, scooting herself back into the seat. Her feet barely reached the floorboard. "But I have to try not to get flat-out hysterical when I do." Her smile was growing.

I waited, checked out the passing cars—*Good grief, look at all the Cadillacs here*—checked out the rearview mirror.

Andie finally turned to me. "She's doing Matt again."

"Prudence?"

"Yes, ma'am."

My jaw hung off its hinges and I stared at her. Someone honked—I'd probably slowed to almost eighty—so I had to pick up my speed and focus on the road.

"You're talking about now?" I asked, eyes firmly facing front.

"Yup."

"Well, they've been in love forever."

"Yeah, but that's not the best part," Andie smirked.

"I'm not going to beg," I said. But I would have.

"Ron wants Eva to be a virgin," she said, the giggles busting out before she was done with the sentence.

"I don't think so," I said. "Not since middle school."

"Don't exaggerate," she said. "She lost it in the ninth grade. And she was probably a late bloomer for steamy old

San Antonio at that. Anyway, you know how it is with Eva. She just likes it. She's *always* liked it. Remember that night when you and me decided it was because she doesn't want to be anything like her frigid mama and Eva said, no, it's because it *feels* good."

"Yeah. She did that sexy, dreamy little dance, looked like she was making love to a warm breeze." I smiled at the memory. I thought at the time, man, if must feel *really* good.

"Ron hasn't wanted to do it for a while," Andie continued, shaking her head. "At least a month. I dunno. Maybe longer."

Nothing about Dr. Sphincter could surprise me. Except maybe this. "According to Matt, Ron told Eva that it would enhance their experience. You know, not doing it anymore. Make it more meaningful on their wedding night. Like it's the first time for both of them. Even though he's a hundred and ten and has two rotten kids." Andie stopped. "That was me, Eva didn't say that."

I figured.

She made her eyes big, getting into the story. "Well, you know Eva. She couldn't *stand* not doing it. So just about this same time, Matt called her up, all despondent about you running off with Brad at the wedding. And that was that. They've been doing it like rabbits ever since. Every chance they get."

"I guess I can't call him Prudence anymore," I said.

"Matt told me he thought at first that maybe they'd get back together, it was so good. But she said no, she's gonna marry Ron. Matt could have her for just this little while or not at all. His choice."

"Somebody's gonna get hurt. I'm betting it won't be Eva."

"I don't know..." Andie said, letting her voice trail. "She's still in love with him."

"Then why are we going to this stupid shower? Why doesn't she just call it off?"

"Have you seen her ring?"

"Five carats does *not* mean true love, Andie. You know it doesn't. If she's still in love with Matt, she needs to break this whole thing off. Love's the *only* thing that matters."

"Think about what you're saying. What would happen if Eva married Matt? He'd be working in some clinic somewhere, trying to solve some huge problem that can't be solved. She'd be stuck at home, no money, no credit cards and zero work ethic. They can't help who they are."

"So why the sphincter? Why can't she find someone else?"

"Have you seen that ring?"

"Andie!"

"I'd marry him."

"You would not," I said, but Andie wasn't listening, busy holding out her left hand, imagining the massive ring there.

By the time we made it down to the country club, it was a few minutes before twelve. Oops. This was not exactly early. I wouldn't have time to do any checking on anything. Ron was waiting on the steps. A tall, thin, unstable volcano.

I got out of the Jeep, held up my hands and willed him to back off, to settle down and get a grip.

The volcano erupted before I'd taken three steps.

"Where the hell have you been?" it spewed.

Andie and I chose to ignore the explosion. Or pretend to. I made a big deal of saying hello to the valet. He was gawking—either at Dr. Sphincter or Andie's legs in her triple-tall slides. Hard to tell with his dark wraparound sunglasses.

The sphincter fumed. It wasn't as noisy, just scarier. As I breezed past him into the somber interior of Dallas's most prestigious club, he said something about me not answering my phone and place cards and screwing everything up. He didn't let up until we'd reached the entrance to the reception room where a few people had already gathered, having their first cocktail of the day. On closer look, maybe it wasn't their first.

I did a quick scan of the room for Brad. Not there. Neither was Eva. "What have you done with her?" I asked, turning to look directly at Ron for the first time since we'd driven up. He was still tall, athletic-looking and tan from all his biking, golf and tennis. The midlife crisis poster child. When Andie and I talked about him being old and wrinkled, we were talking about his soul, not his face. If he wasn't always so mad, he might even have been handsome in a rugged way. Now he was just red. Maybe being a virgin was getting to him.

"You tell me, Miss Organizer," he said through his teeth.

"Is Lauren with her?" I asked. Lauren was Ron's fifteen-year-old daughter. Eva had thought a morning at the spa would bring them closer, let them bond in the algae pit or something. Eva spent a great deal of her down-on-earth time thinking about how she could win the affection of these step-teens. Ron's eighteen-year-old son didn't like Eva, either.

Apparently Ron had decided to stop speaking to me. Part of me thought it was great.

"Look," I said. "Traffic's a nightmare today. She's probably just running late. Go in, be nice to your guests." I was just kidding about that part. "Andie and I'll go wait for her." I was really going out to wait for Brad.

Andie was standing behind me, nodding furiously. The thought of being in that room with all those good old white boys was probably more than she was prepared to take on right then. Or ever. A few of the big ones were getting that look in their eyes like they wanted to come on over and scoop her up.

"It'll be fine," I said as we left. But I felt a twinge, a darkness seeping in from the edges.

We'd gotten halfway down the hall, when the valet caught us.

"Ma'am, you'd better come on out front."

We ran out through the massive front doors back into the blinding October sunshine. All three of us screeched to a stop as we took in the scene.

Eva was sitting in the driver's seat of one of Ron's cars, the Porsche. She could have been an advertisement for any number of Toppo luxury items—the car, the diamond ring, the lime silk outfit, the prominent new boobs. A really provocative and enticing ad. The kind where you don't know what they're selling but you do know that you'd die to have your life be just like that.

But something marred this picture. Another woman—all leathery-brown skin and perky tennis whites—was leaning on the door into the convertible, straining to get her fingers around Eva's neck. It was Dewina, Ron's ex-wife. Eva had pointed her out to me on one of our zillion prewedding reconnoitering trips. Dewina had looked better then, less sinewy, as she sipped her wine at a table surrounded by the other lunching ladies. That had been just after the divorce was final. Maybe she had been still in shock. Or on stratospheric dosages of Zoloft.

Lauren, the step-teen, was standing next to the car on the other side, staging her own little show, screaming and sobbing hysterically. Stamping her feet.

Ron, the chef of this little tossed salad, was nowhere to be seen.

"*Dewina!*" I yelled, running to the car as fast as I could in shoes without backs. I probably looked like a marathoner in the final stretch. One recovering from a recent, debilitating stroke. It took me forever to make it all the way down the steps and across the cobblestone drive.

Dewina was in some kind of homicidal, jilted-wife zone and she wasn't coming out for the wimpy likes of me. It must have been too much for her, seeing her young and incredibly sexy replacement race up with her daughter in tow, to her club, in her former car and wearing a diamond ring the size of a headlight.

Two of the other valets were standing a safe distance away, mumbling "Mrs. Broadhurst, please. Mrs. Broadhurst," as ineffectively as my shouting.

Eva's face was turning an ugly shade of purple. She was keeping herself alive by pushing as hard as she could on Dewina's chin and cheek. With her face twisted to the side, Dewina couldn't get a really good killing grip. Just a hurting one.

"Get Ron!" I hollered, shuffling around to the driver's side.

"I can't find him!" the valet hollered back from the safe distance of the top step.

"Do it!" Andie said to him, in her you-don't-want-to-see-me-mad voice. He ran back inside.

Andie and I reached the Porsche at the same time and we both pulled Dewina from behind, me on one side up high on her shoulders, Andie on the other side down low, on her bent-over hips. "Help us," I shouted to everyone, to anyone. Nobody budged.

We were making a little progress, getting Dewina away, freeing Eva's arms. But Dewina still had all ten fingers wound around Eva's neck. She was stronger than all three of us. She'd probably been whacking a lot of tennis balls lately, pretending they were Ron's genitals.

Eva was able to get herself propped up on her right arm. Just as I was thinking that we'd made it, that we were going to get them separated without anyone dying, over Dewina's shoulder I saw that the delicate Evalina Aguirre-Velasquez had cocked her left arm back, and was curling her pretty long fingers into a ball. I opened my mouth to shout. To shout what?

I didn't get a sound out before Eva's fist slammed into Dewina's face with the power of a wrecking ball, catching her just above her left eye with the magnificent, five-carat diamond. Dewina's head jerked back with a snap and little drops of drool and blood dotted the air in parabolic flight paths around her head. The blow knocked her from my arms and she fell on top of Andie, totally covering her, obliterating everything but narrow ankles and tiny feet in their dark red heels. Blood poured from the wound above Dewina's eye, running down her face and hair in streams.

Ron came running out of the club with the valet and promptly fell down the steps, landing in a heap at the bottom. Lauren pretended to faint. And Brad ran over from the parking lot with a silver and white gift-wrapped box gripped in his hand.

15

WE SAT ON the front steps of the country club, holding hands and watching the last of the cleanup. Any awkwardness he and I might have felt at seeing each other for the first time since my meltdown had been lost in the bedlam and the blood. My dress looked like I'd wandered in front of a firing squad. So much for sane and reserved. That was probably frowned on at the club—sitting on the front steps and being covered in blood, both. But there was no one to notice. The guy who'd been cutting the grass was busy spraying off the driveway with a hose. The valets were redirecting traffic flow, hustling members in and out through the side entrance. All the guests for Eva's shower had mysteriously lost their appetites and left without eating the Provençal luncheon the chef and I had spent so many hours planning. Eva's father and slightly befuddled mother had emerged to take Eva back to Ron's house. Ron left to join them as soon as he could, staying only long enough to get Dewina bandaged and the bleeding stopped. He didn't say goodbye. I gave Andie the keys to my Jeep so she could go get cleaned up and do something about her eye—the one that had gotten an elbow in it when Dewina fell.

A group of Dewina's lunching friends, fresh from their tennis games, had rescued the once-again-noisy step-teen and a couple of them took Dewina to the hospital for stitches. They were all thinking "lawsuit," I could tell. Well, most of them were. Some were thinking murder. Eva should probably avoid the club for a while.

I looked at Brad. "I know what you're thinking," I said.

He turned to me and lifted his eyebrow.

"You wish you were back at work. Getting something important done."

"Nope," he said, and grinned for the first time that day.

"What then? You're awfully quiet."

"I was thinking that that was one helluva left hook. You sure wouldn't want to piss her off if you could help it."

"Yeah," I laughed. "Growing up in San Antonio taught Eva a lot about life." *And sex.* I pushed the thought of her and poor Matt away. "She's not as fragile as she looks."

"And you?" he asked, holding my chin lightly with his fingers. "Are you as fragile as you look?"

I snorted.

You have got to quit doing that!

I didn't mean to snort. I meant it to come out sounding like that little French *ppphhhh* that Eva did.

"What was that for?" he asked, pulling his hand away.

I concocted a fragile little laugh to nullify the snort. "Because I'm tall. Not a bit fragile."

"Delicate," he said, lifting his hand again, but stopping just short of touching my face.

Would kissing on the front steps be frowned upon?

"They're about done here," Brad said, straightening, looking around, taking his hand back. "Let's go get something to eat." He was reeling himself in, again. I could tell.

"I need to go check that the presents are safe and make sure they have all the food boxed up. Eva and Ron have a zillion out-of-town guests—it'll probably come in handy." Then I had a thought. "Hey, you want me to get us some? There's olives, nuts and melons with raw ham, goat cheese, Dijon-crusted salmon—"

His face said, "not my thing." "I know a great barbecue place down in Oak Cliff," he interrupted. "The best. You wouldn't want to be down there at midnight, but it's pretty safe in daylight."

"What about my dress?" I asked, looking down at the blood.

"You haven't been down to Oak Cliff, have you?" he chuckled. "They wear a lot of that down there."

I looked at him like he was serious.

"It's fine," he said. "In the daytime. And this is the best barbecue you will ever eat. I promise. Come on." He stood and pulled me up with him. "You wanna see if they have anything you could wear in the Pro Shop?"

"I can't."

"Why not?"

"It hurts my feelings to overpay for stuff. Especially stuff I don't need."

He just stood there looking at me.

"Weird, huh? The more I hang around Toppos, the worse I get." What was it about this guy that made me babble?

"Toppos?"

I was in it now, might as well swim. "Yeah, that's what I call them. Eva and Ron are both Toppos. You know, Top of the Line. Absolute Top of the Line. Everything they buy has to be really, really expensive. I mean it's okay for some things, but every single thing?" I sighed.

"Toppos," he repeated.

"Does that sound like I'm just jealous? Because I don't think that's it. This wedding has made me want to bargain shop. Or else not buy anything ever again."

"My father must be a Toppo. He appreciates finer things," he said. "Actually, he demands the finest things. Always."

Oops.

He pushed my hair aside and kissed my cheek. "It drives me nuts." And then he hefted the present he'd brought in his left hand. "Toppos, huh? Maybe I'll rethink this."

THE BOY KNEW HIS BARBECUE. I could go on and on about how it tasted with a beer. How spicy it was. And tangy. And just a tiny bit sweet. And so unbelievably tender. But I won't.

"Man, you look great," he said, reaching across the wood plank table for my hands. We'd stopped at a Gap on the way down. I'd found some flare jeans and a wispy little shirt that looked like something my mom would have worn back in the day.

"My shoes don't really go..." I said, looking down at my fancy slides, because I was still, at an ancient twenty-four, unable to graciously accept a compliment.

"This is Dallas, Sky. They're perfect!"

Things were heating up nicely again. I was smart enough to shut up, smile and let Silence do the talking.

Except she didn't get a chance because I had the sudden feeling that something was wrong. And then my phone rang in my purse. I looked across the table at Brad.

"What is it?" he asked.

"I don't know," I said, thinking about Asia for no particular reason.

"Dylan!" Leila sobbed into the phone. An electric buzz raced from the back of my neck down my arms. Leila's like me, she never cries. "Asia's run away."

"What?" I'd just seen her a few hours ago.

It took a long time for me to understand, between Leila's weeping and my total inability to put two intelligent thoughts together. Asia had somehow gotten herself on an early morning flight from Dallas Love Field to Albuquerque.

I reached for Brad with my free hand. He took it and engulfed it with his long, hard fingers, his eyes on my face.

"Leila...Leila," I said, barely above a whisper, trying to quiet her sobs. "Why?"

She slowed down enough so I could catch most of her words. She said that Asia had taken a credit card and gone off to find her daddy. Her real daddy. Last seen somewhere up in Santa Fe. And then she started sobbing again in little jagged bursts. "Something happened, Dylan. At the bus station. A man..."

"Who, Leila? What happened?"

She couldn't answer. I closed my eyes and listened to her weep. I thought about that heavy backpack thumping down the stairs this morning. And how Asia had looked so grown-up. When I opened my eyes again, I saw Brad's worried face. What had he heard me say? A why, a who, a what? I moved the phone away from my mouth. "It's Asia," I told him. "She's gone off to go find her dad in New Mexico."

"Is she okay?" he asked, squeezing my hand even tighter.

I just shook my head and my shoulders did an unhappy shrug.

Leila calmed a little and started talking again. But her voice was empty. "Mother's gone to get her. She knew something was wrong, was already on her way, heading up I-25 when she got the call."

I didn't care what hocus pocus Grandma Frank thought was involved, I was just glad she was there.

"What's she driving?" I asked Leila.

"The convertible," she said, her voice dropping even lower.

Oh, God. It would take her years to get there. If she even made it. Grandma Frank didn't show much sign of wear but the old Mercedes was pooping out fast. She should have taken her truck.

"I'm getting on a plane right now," I said.

"No, no. Don't do that. Mother's bringing her back."

"I need to be with her, Leila," I said and then I had to do the trick with my eyes, looking around, making them big so that no tears would creep out. Brad put my hand to his lips.

"Just wait." She started crying again. It was scary listening to her sobs. Leila and I had both stopped crying, had used up all our tears on Asia's father. Years and years ago.

I tried to drag some air into my lungs. "For how long?"

"I don't know. Grandma Frank's going to try to make the reservations while she's driving. I'll call you."

"Leila?" I said. But she was gone.

"Tell me," Brad said and I looked across the picnic table and knew that it was safe to do so. I could trust him.

And I tried to, but his phone kept ringing. Three times at least. Each time he checked the little screen, apologized then answered it. Things, apparently, were not going well in his absence.

After the last call, I said, "Hey, I've been thinking. You probably..." and then my phone rang. It was Leila again.

"Hi, love. Listen, Asia's fine. Mother is up there with her now," she said, her voice light, happily back on the sunny side. "Asia's not talking much but I think it was just a scare. She and Mother are both exhausted, though, so they're going to stay in Albuquerque tonight and then fly back tomorrow."

"Oh, thank God!" But a little sensation tickled the back of my neck. Would Leila let herself know if something bad had happened? Would Asia risk darkening Leila's world to tell her?

"Dylan," Leila said with a hesitant note in her voice. "What am I going to say to her?"

"Tell her the truth."

"And that is..."

"Tell her he was an asshole." My voice was hard. I looked up to see what Brad thought of the delicate Sky now, but he was watching my face with his mysterious dark eyes and his expression didn't change. Not even an eyebrow.

"But he wasn't," Leila said. "Remember?"

"Yeah," I answered so quietly I could hardly hear myself. I wasn't going to think about that, which was one of those things I was particularly good at. Not thinking about things. Me and Scarlett O'Hara.

"Okay, I'm going to say this really fast before someone's phone rings," I said when I ended the call. "I know you need to get back to work. Could you take me to my Jeep? Andie's got it."

"Is your little sister okay?"

"Yeah, we think so. She's with my grandma."

"Good. Are you going to tell me the story? About her dad?"

"Maybe," I said. I was lying.

His phone rang. He sighed. "Can I still see you tonight?"

"If you can stand the excitement," I said and we gave each other tired little smiles.

It took us more than an hour to get back to my Jeep and Andie.

"You look really good," she said, surprised, as we watched Brad drive away. She didn't need to be *that* surprised.

"I got 'em on sale at the Gap."

"Would you stop that?"

"What?"

"Always telling people how little you pay for stuff," Andie said, shaking her head. "It's as bad as Eva bragging about how much she pays. Your mamas didn't teach y'all about not discussing price?"

Rational thought she might have a point.

"Anyway, I wasn't talking about your clothes. Look at you. You're all shimmery and dewy-eyed," she said. "Why are you here?"

"He needed to get back to work."

"I thought he was taking the whole day off to be with you."

I gave her my ironic look. "Like that was going to happen," I said and explained about all the phone calls. His and mine.

"That Asia is something else! Is she all right?"

I shrugged. I tried to feel what I was feeling, zero in on it, but couldn't quite get it. I shook my head. "I feel like I'm missing something. Maybe I'm just so worried about her."

"She's with your grandma, she's gonna be fine. That old lady is tough."

She was right.

"How do you like my eye?" she asked, pointing and wincing even though she didn't touch it. It was pink and red with a few lilac undertones.

"Beautiful. It looks like one of Asia's paintings. What are you going to do about tonight?"

She did one of her dismissive hand flips. "I had red blotches all over me the whole time I was growing up, till I got outta there. You won't even see this little old thing after I get my makeup on. And what are *you* gonna to do about tonight?"

"What do you mean?"

"I mean the part about you finally sleeping with that beautiful long-legged dude who just dropped you off."

"I don't know, Andie. It's not the right time. I'm so worried about Asia. And he's up to his eyebrows in work." I pictured his eyebrows in my head, the way he could raise just one. "Anyway, we didn't even really get a chance to talk…"

"Not the right time! Do you not feel the heat blasting off you guys? I still haven't recovered from that goodbye kiss and I was just standing here watching."

"But it's this on again, off again thing. I don't know—"

"Listen to yourself! I don't know what kind of shit you're talking, but I am sick of all your excuses. You've been making up reasons your whole life why you can't do this or that. So afraid they're gonna leave you, you don't even give 'em a chance to get there. I got over my rotten childhood and you're going to have to get over yours, too. You can't even talk about it!"

"For your information, I just told Brad about it."

She stopped her lecture right in the middle of a finger shake. "You did?"

I nodded, still giving her my superior stare.

"Well? You feel better? Letting it out?"

No. "There's nothing to let out, Dr. Freud," I said, looking down my nose at her. "Just because I don't go on and on about it. I had it pretty good, you know. I wasn't knocked around like you were or abused or anything. Everybody has junk."

"We're getting off topic, here," Andie said, all huffy again. "If you're so damn over it, why are you still a virgin?"

"As if you didn't know. It's just never been right."

"And you're the math person! What are the odds? Not one single right time in all these years? You're just scared."

"Am not."

"Well, then, make love with that gorgeous man, dupe."

I gave her my Mona Lisa smile.

"Dupe," she said.

"You heard from Eva?" I asked.

"No. You?"

My phone rang. "That's her." I dragged my cell out for

the millionth time. Andie held her ear to it so she could hear, too. Except I hadn't pressed the talk button yet.

"Eva, hi," I said, after I'd finally gotten it pushed with Andie hanging on my arm.

"Hello, yourself," she said, sounding even more cloud-bound than usual.

"How are you?" I asked.

"I'm fine. How are you?" I wondered if she'd already spaced out the luncheon disaster. Eva didn't dwell on the unpleasant.

"Is anything broken? Or hurt?" Andie shouted into the phone. And my ear. "Like your hand?"

"Nothing," Eva whispered. And then made a soft little echo, "Nothing, nothing, nothing, nothing..."

"At all?"

"At all." She sounded eerily like her pill-popping mom. "At all, at all, at all..."

"How's Ron?" I broke in.

"I like Ron," she announced, voice firming. "I don't know why you don't. You and Andie are so mean. Mean. *Méchante.*"

She hadn't completely lost it; she was still speaking French.

"Are you drugged up, Eva?" Andie shouted again.

I gave her the phone so I didn't have to listen to her hollering. Or to Eva's echoes. I leaned back on my Jeep, closed my eyes and caught some warm October rays on my face. And thought about Brad.

Some while later, Andie put the phone in my hand. It was going to need another recharge soon. As was I.

"What a wreck," Andie sighed. "Her mom gave her some pills to relax."

"We're all wrecks," I said.

"I," Andie informed me, smoothing out her skirt, "am not a wreck." Silence and I checked out her eye.

"Why don't they just cancel tonight?" I asked, face back to the sun, thinking of things I'd rather be doing in Brad's after-work hours.

"You're kidding right?"

No, that was Wishful. "Are you still taking the new guy?"

"Terrell? Yeah. Why?"

"Just asking."

"Why wouldn't I?" Andie asked, searching my face. "I'm sure not going there alone. You people scare me when you bunch up like that in groups."

"Well…" I said, serenely ignoring the "you people" thing, those two little words that get everybody all riled up, no matter which "you people" you're talking to. "I don't think makeup is gonna fix that eye. It's not red anymore. It's black. And blue. And swollen." Andie ran into the house.

I took the tollway back to Leila's house. There was no other way to get up there, not if you wanted to arrive on the same day you left. I drove in robot mode and wondered what Brad thought about my crazy family. And all the stuff I'd told him. Andie made it sound as if my childhood was some big trauma like hers had been. It wasn't. A little lonesome, maybe. But at least it had taught me to be realistic, not get my hopes up too high. That way, when people left you didn't get hurt.

I called Grandma Frank. Asia picked up. "Hey," she said. "I knew it was you."

"Hey back." I could hear the relief in my voice. "Whatzup?"

"Not much. Just hangin' with the Grams." I could hear Grandma Frank say something in the background and Asia giggled. I took my first deep breath in hours.

"Are you okay?"

"Yeah. I'm okay."

"Really? You're not just being brave?"

Silence breathed into the phone. But that didn't mean anything. Asia didn't answer superfluous questions.

"When do you get back tomorrow?" I asked.

"I don't know yet if I'm coming back."

"What do you mean? You have to!"

"I can't, Dylan," she said in a grown-up voice I hadn't heard before. "I gotta find him. I'm *going* to find him. Grandma Frank might help me." She was talking to her then, not me.

"But, Asia, you guys are all coming to the wedding on Saturday!" I heard the desperation in my voice. But only Silence answered. And it had been a stupid thing to say. Pretty trivial compared to the stuff she was dealing with. "Asia Cézanne. Come home. I'll help you find him, I promise, little one. Just come home."

"I can't, Dylan. I'm sorry, and I love you, but I can't."

And she was gone before I knew it.

16

RATIONAL HAD DECIDED long ago that spending any brain time on Asia's father was a colossal waste. So I didn't. Despite my smug response to Andie, it's hard to explain, then, why I'd told Brad about him as he drove me back up to my Jeep from the barbecue place. I'd rather have been talking about us. Or the traffic. Or, God, anything else.

"So what's the deal about Asia's dad?" he'd asked. I considered my options. Like jumping out a window. We were crawling along the tollway. Crisscrossing Dallas on a weekday afternoon was an inefficient way to spend the time.

I took a deep breath. "Well, his name was Drew. He was like my fourth father." *So let's talk about something else.*

"Fourth! How old were you?"

"Ten, I think." I tried to figure out how old I'd been, which I usually did by counting off the various men who had filled the father role in my life. But that method of counting invited too much lingering along memory lane, and, today, I just wasn't up for it.

"So Asia's dad…"

Guess I'd let the silence drag on too long. "Yeah. Drew. Great name for an artist, huh? He was good, too. A couple of galleries carried his stuff."

"He named her after another artist, Cézanne?"

I shrugged. "Why am I telling you this?" I asked. "Boring. We should be talking about other stuff." I steamed up the words so he'd know what I meant.

"It's some story," the reigning champion of Restraint said, avoiding talk of any of that other stuff. Like us.

I guess I could have turned the tables and grilled him. *So, Brad, darling, what's the deal here? Is this the real thing or not?* But even *I* knew love's best not discussed with a baseball bat. I decided to just tell him the stupid story and get it over with. I took another deep breath.

"Leila and I had just left Two Step. That was my name for my second stepfather. He had fiscal issues—for every two steps forward, there were three back. Anyway, we left him to his shopaholic ways and spent some time drifting, living with friends." I paused, remembering how stressed I'd felt, how anxious we'd never have a home. Leila, on the other hand, had thrived.

"You know, if you asked my mom she'd probably tell you that was her all-time favorite summer. She was free."

"And you?" he asked. "What did you think?" He was hearing gaps in the story, catching sight of that sad little girl.

"I could have been happy if I'd just let myself," I said. "I was so afraid I'd be one of those pathetic homeless kids when I started my new school. The ones they gave free breakfasts to." I made my voice dramatic. "Can you even imagine anything worse?" *Yeah, not having any friends, anyone to talk to.*

He looked over at me.

"So, anyway," I breezed on, "it was time for school and the free breakfasts. We were still just drifting along, hanging out. Wherever. Then one day my mom came back from an interview in Santa Fe, hair all tucked up tight in a bun, announcing she'd gotten a job. A really great job."

"Doing what?"

"Senior Systems Analyst."

"Wow. I wouldn't have guessed that."

"Yeah. In my family we call it the miraculous marketability of technical proficiency. It's a religion." She was going to be the only female in the department. She said they needed her skills so badly they'd decided to forgive her her vagina. Leila had to say stuff like that; she was liberated.

"I'm sorry," I said. "I'm rambling." I looked at the side of his chiseled face wondering what he was thinking.

He stared out over the jam of parked cars. "Doesn't look like we're going anywhere soon." We'd moved maybe fifty yards since I last looked, hadn't even cleared the Galleria.

"Do you ever go there, to the Galleria?"

"Too Toppo for me," he laughed. "So she's got a job now..."

"Yeah, and she found us a place to live." She'd hit up Grandma Frank for the first-last-and-deposit and we'd moved in. "It was this teeny, run-down place just outside of Santa Fe, up in Tesuque. Perched on a hill, a tall adobe wall around it. There were only four little rooms, but they'd been freshly plastered and white-washed before we moved in. You could see the outlines of the adobes in the walls. And we had this courtyard full of sunflowers and four different colors of hollyhocks. That first night we lay out there, on an old tablecloth, breathing mountain air and counting falling stars." Just me and Leila. Home at last.

I looked over, to see if I'd gotten carried away.

"You make it sound magic."

"The Land of Enchantment," I whispered and let myself feel what it had been like. "So," my smile faded, "the magic lasted exactly thirteen days. And, surprise, surprise, another guy moved in." The basic, immutable laws of life: nature hates a vacuum; night follows day; and Leila's gonna have her a man.

"Had she known him long?" Which was one of the things I liked about Brad. He asked reasonable questions.

"She'd just met him. I'm sure there was a day or two of

courtship leading up to it but there couldn't have been very many."

Brad gave me a long look and I hunched my shoulders. And then I remembered that guys always think you're going to turn out like your mother. "That's the way it was back then. You know? Easy love. She's quite respectable now."

"Was this Drew?" Brad asked. And his phone rang.

Yeah, Drew. And I'd hated him. From the very first. Hated him for all the things he was and wasn't. But mostly I hated him because I was supposed to. It's in the rulebook for step-kids.

Nobody cared. Leila had Drew. Drew had Leila. The dogs liked him and I was quiet in my hatefulness.

I glanced at Brad, still up to his dark eyebrows in conversation. Good. We could drop all this.

Except I couldn't. The door had splintered open.

Leila had been in heaven. She had her job, a nest, a man, the dogs and me—not necessarily in that order of priority. Watching them, I'd sit there thinking my hateful thoughts and wonder if she was going to hook this one. Drew made it clear to anyone who'd listen that he never wanted to get married and certainly never wanted children. Period. He'd gotten a vasectomy when he was still pretty young. And he'd never regretted it. Not for a second. Hardly promising for the serial bride.

But every day after school, Drew would put up his painting in the garage, clean his brushes and walk down with the dogs to the end of the dirt road to meet me at the bus. He must have thought I'd be easy like Leila. No way. He was nothing to me. Less than nothing. I'd get down the steps of the bus, say "hi" to the dogs, then quietly go my way as though he wasn't there.

I waited for him to tire of the game and leave me alone.

But every day he was there at the end of the road, acting not particularly happy to see me, but there all the same.

And one day I forgot to hate him. Actually, it didn't happen all in one day. I'd already started trying to see him as the bus turned the corner, to see if he'd have on his old cowboy hat or just his sunglasses. And which of his three shirts he'd be wearing. But that day—I remember it had been a pretty rough day, Santa Fe public schools were no picnic—I found myself sitting on that hot, dusty bus hoping he'd be there. And knowing that he wouldn't be just because now I'd let myself need him. But he was in all his long-haired, blue-jeaned beauty. The most constant thing I'd had in my whole crazy life.

Brad was still on the phone. He glanced over at me and did an apologetic little shrug. I just smiled at him, lost in those enchanted days with Drew.

It turned out I wasn't so tough. When I finally tumbled, I fell harder for him than Leila had. She hadn't tried to resist.

I'd watch him standing there as the bus pulled up, dark hair blowing in his eyes, a denim shirt thrown over his T-shirt, sleeves rolled up, hands tucked into the pockets of his paint-splattered jeans. The dogs would be dancing at his feet. And I'd want to shout with the pure pride of ownership. See that guy, that amazing-looking guy there? He's with us!

He never missed a day but I'd hold my breath anyway, until we'd turned the corner and I could see him and my heart would do its little backflip. Then I'd get off the bus and he'd say, "Hey" and I'd say, "Hey" and I'd hug the dogs and we'd go off and do wonderful New Mexico mountain things. Like hide and seek with Alfred, the hound dog, who could always sniff you out no matter where you hid. Or hike and search for caves or old mining camps. Then we'd wander home, my backpack, bursting at the seams with homework, perched high on his back. When we got close, we'd race to the turquoise gate. Alfred always won. We'd wolf down homemade granola cookies and raw milk at our round kitchen table and wait for Leila to get home from work so we could tell her about our day.

"I am really sorry," Brad said as he put down his phone. "I just feel bad about taking you away from work today."

"Don't. 'Cause you're not. I'm never away."

Admitting you have a problem is the first step to recovery. "Does that ever bother you?"

"You kidding? I'm doing exactly what I want. It's great."

"You've taken on so much, though."

"My dad, at my age, had already made his first million."

That explained a lot.

"Look. The traffic's starting to move. Finish your story. This new guy was Drew, right?" He put his hand on my leg.

"I didn't think guys ever listened," I cooed. "You're the first one I've met who actually hears stuff."

"Don't be hard on us guys. We try." He squeezed my leg and took his hand back to change lanes. "So...tell me."

I wanted the hand back. "At first I didn't like Drew, but he won me over. Best dad I ever had."

"What happened?"

"Leila got pregnant with Asia," I said. Poor Leila. She'd led a charmed life. Except for that part about birth control. It was as if no method could counteract those Earth Mother genes. I was the failed Pill baby, Grey the leaky condom and Asia the incomplete vasectomy. "And Drew didn't want a baby."

"Oh."

"Yeah. Oh. And *poof*, he was gone." Wasn't there waiting for me at the bus stop. Wasn't anywhere.

"So Asia's never even seen her dad?"

"Nope."

"Well, what..." And the phone rang.

Thank goodness. The story was over. Leila and I had cried and cried until there weren't any tears left. Then she told herself that she'd never really wanted him. He was this and that and some other bad thing. The next guy would be different. Oh, joy. Like that's what *I* wanted. She threw herself back into her busy life, exploding tummy and all—working, waiting for the baby. Searching for that next empty lap.

And I died inside. Shut down and strung yellow police tape around the entrances. And there was nothing more to say.

17

WHEN I GOT BACK up to Leila's house I had less than two hours to get ready. To not be my usual fifteen minutes late.

Grey ran to the door and hugged me as soon as I walked in. "Sis!" he cried into my waist. "Asia's gone to New Mexico. She's staying with Grandma Frank at a fancy hotel. We think she's okay, right?" He leaned his head back to look at me, still holding tight to my legs. "Right?"

"I don't know, Grey. I hope so," I said and hugged him.

He spun away from me and plopped himself down on the bottom stair. Then he looked up with a red, miserable face. "Am I just worried or do I think something's really wrong?"

I sat down next to him. "I wish I knew, little one," I whispered and put my arm around his shoulder again.

Grey wasn't used to these kinds of upsets in his seamless suburban world. "Why does she have to find that other guy, anyway?" he asked. "Why isn't Daddy enough?"

Oh, let me count the ways.

I didn't have to answer because Leila came around the corner then and I stood to hug her. Grey did, too, standing on the bottom stair for height, and started to sob.

"Oh, no!" Step Away groaned as he came out of his library into the foyer. The three of us jumped as though we'd been standing on a trampoline. "Dylan, goddammit. Don't get everybody all riled up again. We've been over and over this. Asia's fine. She's been naughty and she'll be punished when she gets back, but right now she's fine." He turned to go back into his dark faux-leathered room. "So everybody give it a rest."

I looked into Leila's bloodshot green eyes. And I saw my old enemy Fear. Or maybe it was Panic.

Grey stopped snuffling and we all closed our eyes. I know I did. I felt Leila's shoulder slump, heard her take a deep breath and start to pull away, to follow Grant into the icy caves of the Step Freeze. But I pulled her back and kissed her cheek and we looked at each other a moment before I let her go in there alone. And then I kissed Grey and crept upstairs to leave them to it. Because if I knew anything, I knew there was one person in the world who could make it worse. And that someone was me.

Upstairs, I sat down at the computer and wasted another fifteen minutes I didn't have writing one of my poems.

Asia And Me
Fathers I've had = three or four
Fathers I wanted = one
Fathers she wants = just one more
Fathers she's had = none

I didn't save it—risking the tremendous loss to future generations—because it was Grant's computer and it was always innocent things like this that brought down whole corporations when they were discovered lurking out there on the hard disc. Imagine what it could do to a little patched-together family.

I showered and dressed and even piled my hair up in a loose French roll. Then in a burst of cosmetic overachievement, I put on my makeup at the house, instead of on the freeway, like usual. I was thinking every detail through, plotting, planning it. But the effort wasn't for the out-of-towners' dinner, for all of Eva's aristocratic relatives from somewhere else. *Tonight is the night. The night of nights.* With each passing year, the possibility for romantic spontaneity decreased. By the time I was thirty, I was going to have on-line project graphs, spreadsheets and supporting documents for it.

I wore my new slinky bias-cut black dress with the asymmetrical hemline because it made me look skinny and French. Okay, maybe only skinny. All right, all right. Jeez. Skinnier.

I was fifteen minutes late. But then so was Andie. Actually, I beat her by a good five. But when she stepped through the front door of Le Bistro, I could see she'd used those minutes well. There was no sign of the black eye. Just that incredible red hair floating around her face, framing the best set of lips in Dallas. Wine-colored dress and the highest-heeled gold sandals I'd ever seen. Good thing I wasn't short. I'd have killed myself in those shoes.

Andie and I got busy trying to make everything perfect for Eva, to make up for the luncheon fiasco. But we couldn't. All those dark-eyed French guys running around had already done it. Out on the patio where the drinks would be served, you couldn't have asked for a better night. Except in a perfect world there wouldn't have been a view of the Hard Rock Café across the way. But Dallas wasn't Paris and that's what you got.

Andie's brand-new boyfriend, Terrell, arrived next. And while he has keeling over at the sight of Andie in her dress, I had time to check him out. There's a word for guys like that: *whoa!* He was big, of course. But that was a given. Andie's formula was: soul mate = big + gentle + understanding + rich. Which pretty much accounted for why *she* was still single. She liked them big to offset her teeny genes and she'd had enough of cruel, stupid and poor to last several lifetimes.

The guests started to arrive and Eva still hadn't shown. Maybe I'd gotten too caught up in the necessity for perfection, but that seemed a bit remiss. It didn't bother Andie. She fell into character, with her stage-speak voice and accompanying elegant gestures. "Hello and welcome. I'm Andie and this is Dylan, Eva's friends. She and Ron have been delayed but they'll be here shortly. We can show you out to the patio bar..." And then I'd take the next group. Terrell stood behind us. I could tell other women had the same thought I did when they saw him. Who wouldn't? Maybe Andie. She was probably more interested in the shape of his portfolio.

I got back from a patio run and Brad was standing there in the Parisian-muraled foyer, talking to Andie and Terrell, Texas-style—as if he'd known them all his life. He wore a suit with a dark shirt and tie. Easy, confident. Like any successful young executive. Except for the longish hair. *And that grin.*

"Wow," he whispered and gave me his I-love-you kiss. I *know* that's what it said. And then he said, "Wow," again.

From that second we entered another world. Coupledom. It was as if we were in a bubble and everything had to first pass through that shield of togetherness. I knew all about couple bubbles. I'd spent enough time on the other side of them.

Andie felt it, too. How could you not? "Why don't you two go back and visit with all those nice folks out on the patio," she said to me, all but nudging and winking, giving us a little time together. "Terrell and I can handle this, can't we, baby?" She had to bend her head all the way back just to see his face.

We'd walked just a short way down the corridor when he stopped and pulled me into the little cutout area for the phone, pressing my naked back against the cool plaster wall. His crooked grin was gone. "My God, you're so beautiful," he said in his rumbley voice. He held himself above me, hands alongside my head, arms rigid, body taut. Fire whooshed through my veins. He let his arms slowly bend, leaned his body into mine and covered my mouth with his, sucking me in.

"We've wasted too much time," he said, lips on my throat.

And then we kissed some more.

When it got to the point where we were seriously going to have to get a room, we pulled apart, straightened each other's rumpled clothing and tried to fake an air of innocence as we drifted in our bubble toward the patio, holding hands. We managed to squeeze in a couple more quick kisses en route. The place was packed. Andie had been busy.

"Where's Eva?" Brad asked. "I wanna meet that left hook."

"I don't think she's here yet," I said looking around.

The eyebrow went up. "Are we worried?"

I smiled at him. "Very."

Andie and I had just decided to have the hostesses take everyone into the dining room when a burst of loud chatter made us all turn to look. Eva's dad stood between Eva on one arm and his wife on the other. They could have been a painting, modern day royals, tall and slim with their ivory skin and raven hair. Except the artist would have had to paint little *X*'s for Eva's mother's eyes. The lady was gone, standing erect simply from habit. Eva's father cleared his throat—does that ever work?—and waited patiently until someone hit a spoon against a glass and got everyone to shut up. Then he started in on his speech, a wistful throwback to an old world of formality and gentle manners. The guy had liked being rich.

"Dear ones, friends and family, thank you for coming to Dallas to celebrate with us the happy occasion of our daughter Eva's marriage. We welcome you and extend our sincerest apologies for not being here upon your arrival. There has been, however, a slight family emergency. Our future son-in-law, the esteemed Dr. Broadhurst, has had a minor mishap, a sprained ankle—do not trouble yourselves, it was nothing more. He was unable to stand without a great deal of pain. We insisted he miss this dinner tonight in order to save himself for the important standing he must do on Saturday at the church." There was a scattering of polite laughter. "And now, may I present to you the bride-to-be, our beautiful Evalina Marie."

All eyes turned on Eva, or maybe they'd been on her the whole time. Mine had. She wore her black hair piled on her head and wrapped with a silver rope, three times around, like the Grecian women did. And she was wearing her nightie. Or maybe she'd just forgotten to put her dress on over her slip. Or, knowing Eva, it was the latest style from Paris and was supposed to look that way.

She stood there, chin slightly lifted, a goddess. Ethereal, ephemeral and, in the flickering light of the patio candles, almost translucent. She wore diamond studs in her ears— huge solitaires that I hadn't seen before—to match her magnificent ring. They caught the light and turned it into radiance, like she'd chosen stars to adorn her body that night. She stayed on her father's arm and started to speak. But unlike her father she didn't need to wait for the crowd to quiet; no one even exhaled.

She cooed in her softest sighing voice, taking long breathy pauses between each phrase, "*Bon soir*. I am so...happy you've joined us...some of you from far, far away..." I thought we were going to lose her then, her thoughts drifting away to those far-off places. We waited and still no one breathed. But she came back and sent a tiny smile to the crowd. "Let me speak with each of you now... personally...so we can become acquainted...or reacquainted...for there are some of you...whom I have not seen...since I was a tiny, little girl... And...in the meantime, *bienvenue*. Our warmest...Texas...welcome...to y'all." The whole place burst into applause.

"That's not the same Eva as this afternoon," Brad said. "Couldn't be."

Eva and her family made their way over to us, with Eva's mom dragging in sideways. Eva focused her Cleopatra eyes on Terrell, then Brad and said, "Ooh. Do I know you?"

I couldn't tell if she was still drugged or not. She always acted this way.

We made all the introductions and she came firmly back on earth for just a minute, turning her head so we could see both dazzling earrings. "Ron got me them this afternoon."

"And where is the darling man?" Andie asked. She didn't make up names like I did, but she got the same message across.

Eva ignored the tone—or maybe she really was drugged and it sailed past her. "He hurt his ankle when he fell down the steps this afternoon, but he'd made up his mind he was going to get these for me," she reached up with her fairy fingers and touched both earrings. "To make up for... everything."

Eva's dad broke in. "Each one is two and a half carats of unflawed perfection," he crowed. Had it been Eva talking, I'd have asked if there was such a thing as flawed perfection but I just smiled at him. Proud fathers are rare in my world. He smiled back and said, "I'm going to have to get Eva a bodyguard if he gives her any more of these huge stones."

I callously calculated the price tag: murderous ex-wife +

spoiled step-kid = 5 more carats. Brad was watching me, his ironic grin in place. So he wasn't a diamond man.

Le Bistro's hostess found me and reminded us that we were already an hour past schedule. Andie obligingly projected her loudspeaker voice at the gathering guests. "Shall we dine?"

Dr. Aguirre sighed, secured a better grip on his wife's elbow and began towing her toward the dining room.

"Would you mind if these two scrumptious men escorted ~~me to the table~~?" Eva asked us. "I hate walking in alone."

Andie and I exchanged amused glances. Eva couldn't help herself. She just adored males. Like my mom.

"Enjoy," we said. Scrumptious young men were rare in Eva's world. And then I remembered Matt.

"Don't move," Brad said, lightly kissing my neck just under my ear. "I'll be right back."

Our couple-bubble stretched to accommodate the distance, keeping us linked as he took Eva's arm. He turned to look back and sent me one of his grins.

We watched them walk off with the silky Eva between them.

"Do you think she's still drugged?" I asked Andie.

"Hard to tell. That was pretty smooth."

Brad was back in a flash, talking quietly into his phone. I waited with him. We were the last ones in the dining room.

Dinner was spectacular. All through the escargot, the duck confit, the beet and pear salad and the sesame-crusted tuna, Brad and I stayed in our couple pod, pressing our legs together, resting hands on thighs, touching arms and fingers whenever the opportunity arose. And sometimes when it didn't. We weren't properly social to our table neighbors but there was only room for two in our pod.

I ate ~~no more than three bites. No snail~~ breath for this night.

But somewhere deep, in the realist corner of my brain, a thought was growing that it wouldn't happen, that Brad would get called away and we wouldn't get together. Not tonight or ever. He'd leave tomorrow morning, our love unloved. There'd always be something keeping us apart. I ruthlessly ignored the thought.

We'd arranged to have the dessert and coffee served out on the candlelit patio, where the stainless steel heat lamps were still keeping everything toasty. A glowing end to a pleasant evening. The guests began to make their leisurely exit from the dining room, happily stuffed and glad to be moving.

Brad and I plotted our getaway.

We hung back as everyone filed out, waiting to make our break. And miracle of miracles, his phone didn't ring.

It vibrated.

I stood off to the side, waiting for him to finish. It provided Eva's dad the perfect opportunity to pounce.

"Dylan, thank heaven you're still here," Dr. Aguirre said. "My service contacted me. I must take a call from a patient." He didn't really practice anymore, but still had a few hangers-on.

And before I could graciously decline, he'd unloaded his wife on me and, with a little bow, disappeared around a corner.

I was too surprised to respond. Brad got off his phone, eyebrow up in the air. Tonight was never going to happen.

Mrs. Aguirre was dead weight. Her husband must have been keeping her pumped up with the sheer force of his will and when he removed it she simply deflated. Brad took her other arm and helped me haul her out onto the patio. We didn't let her into our bubble, just kept giving each other amused glances over the top of her head. We got her into the first chair that presented itself, but she kept listing, just like the dead guy in *Weekend at Bernie's.* Come to think of it, she had the same little Bernie-smirk on her face.

"Could you go get Andie or Eva?" I asked Brad. "I'll stay here and make sure she's okay." Of the two jobs, he was quite pleased with the one I'd assigned him.

Mrs. Aguirre mumbled something. I ignored her, trying to keep Brad in sight.

She sat up rigid in the chair, holding both hands out in front of her, like she was admiring jewels. But her fingers were bare. "I used to love diamonds," she said loudly, so I'd have to pay attention. I did. And so did all the other guests within shouting distance. But their glances only flicked at us and then away. These erudite folks knew how to avoid an embarrassment when it presented itself. Or maybe they were used to her.

"Mmm-hmm," I murmured idiotically. "Diamonds are nice."

"*Nice?*" she shrieked. I bent down to quiet her. "*Nice? They're killing my babies!*"

"Mrs. Aguirre, it's okay. It's okay. Shh."

"*It's* not *okay.*"

"Please. Please. Shh." But despite my efforts, she kept yelling about her babies.

Eva and Andie got there at the same time. They couldn't shut her up, either. She was gone, wild-eyed, some dreadful hallucination scraping at her brain.

"*Maman. Maman.* It's me, Eva," Eva cried, trying to grab hold of her mother's fluttering hands.

Brad came out of nowhere and swooped Mrs. Aguirre up out of the chair into his arms. "You know about blood diamonds, don't you, ma'am?" he asked, gently, respect in his voice.

She was too surprised at being airborne to respond.

He let her legs slide down so she was standing, propped

up by his arm. He kept talking to her the whole time, in his soft, rumbley voice. "You're right. About the diamonds. What's happening down in Sierre Leone and Angola. The warlords using diamonds to buy drugs and then trading the drugs for weapons. They'll do anything to get those diamonds, won't they, Mrs. Aguirre?"

She leaned into him, sobbing and nodding at his soothing voice.

Dr. Aguirre emerged from the restaurant and addressed the horrified group of us—as if his wife wasn't frothing a foot away. "It's going to be a full day again tomorrow. We must say goodbye, now. Come, Eva, help me take your mother to the car." Andie looked up at Brad, shaking her head. "You should do this rescue thing for a living," she said.

Yeah, right, Andie. That's just what he needs. Another job.

18

BRAD AND I left right after the Aguirres. He leaned against his BMW and held out his arms to me. I stepped in between those long, hard legs and pretty soon the question of what we were going to do was all settled and we hadn't had to say a word.

"Follow me?" he asked, and I nodded.

So my phone rang. "I think it's my mom," I said. Damn it. He nodded, looked away and waited.

"What?" I asked. I hadn't meant it to come out like that.

She didn't answer.

"Leila?"

"I left," she said so softly I could hardly hear her.

It was my turn not to answer. *Left Step Away? That's good, right?* Rational wasn't sure, remembering the untethered Leila.

"I'm done," she said with eerie calm. "I walked out."

"Oh."

"But I didn't bring anything with me. My purse or phone..."

"Where are you?"

"I'm at the Starbucks," she whispered. "It's hard to talk. They let me use the phone and have a coffee. Till you get here."

"Leila, I can't." *What kind of a daughter are you?*

"Oh," she murmured, thinking about it. "Well, then..."

"Could you call one of your friends?"

"No. The whole neighborhood would know about it in an hour." And they probably would. The 'burbs were pretty boring.

"Go back home, Leila. Talk to him." Back to Step Hell.

"Never. But don't worry, I'll think of something."

She'd never asked for help before. Not once. "Could you..."

"Not to worry..."

"Wait, I'll come. But can I just drop you off somewhere?"

"That's fine, love. Just bail me out of Starbucks."

I closed my eyes and heard Brad chuckle. "You're leaving, right?"

I drove up to Suburbanville and realized I didn't know which Starbucks. There were four within easy walking distance of her house. I ruled out the one inside Target and found her at the third one. Could these places be more different than Skinny's? I got a stab of homesickness for Austin.

She was sitting in the corner, in one of the only two upholstered chairs in the place. A man was sitting in the other chair, leaning forward, talking to her. The tilt of his body said, "Take me, I'm yours."

I ordered a venti latte at the counter, paid for both our drinks and waited by the counter watching them. This had to break all previous records for finding a new guy.

"Here she is," Leila said, jumping up to hug me. "Dylan, this is Greg Overby. He's just bought one of my houses."

"Nice to meet you, Dylan," he said, shaking my hand, barely glancing at my slinky outfit. "I was just telling Leila that her faux painting sold the house. We fell in love with walls, if that's possible. She should be doing gallery exhibits."

"We always say her talent's too big for canvas," I said, smiling and wishing him away.

"So nice meeting you, Greg," Leila said, dismissing him for me. "And tell your wife I'm thrilled that she likes the mural."

"Not likes, loves..." It took him five more minutes to leave.

I sank into the vacated chair and took a huge sip. I liked my coffee superhot. If you sucked in enough air, it didn't burn your tongue. The trick was to not make disgusting noises in the process. It was lukewarm. Blech. "You're a man-magnet," I said.

"He recognized me. They had my picture in the literature for the Parade of Homes," she laughed, knowing what I'd said was true. "What are you doing? I thought you were racing away."

I just looked at her.

"I see." And I thought she probably did.

"Tell me about Grant," I said. "What made you leave?"

"I'd have thought you, above all, would know that."

She had a point. Except... "But he's been good for you. Ol' Rock Gibraltar." I couldn't believe I was defending him. But what about Grey? How could he handle the childhood I'd had?

"Grant doesn't even understand that he doesn't understand."

"Did you talk to him?" *Right! Could you talk to that man?*

She made a face.

"Did you tell him you were leaving?"

"No," she said. Her voice cracked but she took a deep breath and went on. "Grey was asleep and Grant was in our bedroom watching TV when it was time to leave. I couldn't go in and get my purse so I just left."

"Why was it time to leave?" Did she have a breakup schedule?

"It just was. I could feel it."

Oh. "What about Grey?"

"My head's going to explode," she said looking out the front window onto a major intersection. There was nothing to see, no hills or lakes or parks like in Austin. Just cars.

"You know, the beauty of a place can seep into your soul. Maybe it's the ugliness out here that's gotten to you."

"It's time for a change," she said to the window, nodding. She sucked in a huge breath. "Grey will be fine. Look at you."

Oh, yeah, right. Miss Wella Justed, the ninety-year-old virgin. "And what about Asia?"

"She'll be fine, too." *Wish it and it will be true.* "I'm going to call in the morning. See what the deal is, if they're coming back. If not, I'm flying out there." She sighed. "I keep having this strangling feeling. Something's still wrong."

"Yeah," I said, "I know."

"I hate all this."

"Let's go," I suggested. "We can drive around. Talk."

She nodded and I dumped my cold coffee in the trash along with all the hopes I'd had for this night of nights.

We got in my Jeep and began an aimless drive through a grid of unchanging scenery, like those low-budget cartoons where the car keeps passing the same background over and over.

"Did I ruin it for you with Brad? Calling you up here."

"No. You saved me."

She waited for the explanation.

"He'd been getting phone calls all day. His people couldn't pull some critical reports. And he needs them for his meeting. Today of all days, he should have been in his office."

"But he chose to be with you."

"Yeah. Probably regrets it. Your call gave him his exit strategy. He was almost gone before we got off the phone."

"So how did that save you?" she asked.

"Because he has zero time for anyone in his life. That's why he was dating Miss Hot Links. If you hadn't called, he'd have slept with me tonight. Just because."

"That would have been so bad?" Obviously not in her world.

"It would be nice if it meant something. Not a heat and serve."

"But maybe that's exactly what you need," she said. "This whole virgin thing is dragging you down."

"Yeah, probably so. But I can't. I need it to be real."

"When you find out what that is, you let me know. Okay?"

"I thought you didn't care for reality."

"I don't. But you know me. I hate to miss anything."

We continued driving aimlessly.

"That's what I need," she said, her voice barely audible.

"What's that?"

"An exit strategy," she laughed. "What do you think?"

"I think you should bring your damn purse."

"Yeah. I'm exhausted. How about taking me to one of these plastic hotels? I'll sort this out tomorrow."

"Pick one," I said, pointing. There were five just on that one street. "Maybe I'll stay with you, if that's okay. I'm not staying at Grant's without you and I want to sleep for years."

My phone rang. The evil thing could sense what I wanted, had sacrificed its batteries in making sure I didn't get it.

But when I realized it was Grey, I got over myself. Looked like I would be at Grant's without Leila after all.

19

I SNEAKED INTO the house as quietly as I could, pressing the door handle down as I closed the door so there wouldn't be any loud clicking sounds. In a movie he would have been standing there—secretly, evilly, waiting for me in the gloom. And I would have jumped six feet straight up in the air, and screamed.

He was and I did.

So when I could breathe again, I said, "Grant."

And he said, "Dylan."

I had to get past him and dart up the stairs to check on Grey.

Except he asked, "Do you want some coffee? A cappuccino?"

Who'd want coffee at that hour in the morning?

Me.

"Yes, please," I said in my sweet voice. Whatever game this guy was playing, I was going to be better. "Is Grey up?" I asked his back. "He called a little while ago. He read Leila's note."

"Probably gone back to sleep," Grant said, turning around and looking at me. I mean, really looking. "Or he'd have pounced on you when you came in. I'll start this and then go check."

Whew! I'd have to be sharp. Where was Step Away? Lurking somewhere beneath this conciliatory facade?

He made a quick trip up the stairs and found Grey asleep

on the floor of the playroom. Grant didn't wake him, just came back down and got the cappuccinos all frothed up and steamy.

"Let's go in the living room and drink these," he said. "I like it in there and we never seem to use it."

I get it. Aliens had eaten his brain and this was just a Grant-shell, with an extraterrestrial inside pushing the levers.

"Is Leila okay?" he asked when we'd gotten settled.

I took my first silent sip of hot coffee and air. Heaven. "She's fine. She just needs some time to pull things together."

"She said in her note that she was leaving."

"Yeah. That's what she says."

"You know, we've never even had a real argument before. Ten years of marriage, one disagreement and she wants to leave."

He was talking to me as if we did this all the time. Weird. "We're not very good problem-solvers. More like freak-and-run."

"I thought I understood her."

"Well, she's pretty upset about Asia. We all are."

"I'm upset, too."

"Yeah, but not in the same way. I heard you. You're mad." And Miss Manners refrained from adding, *as usual.*

"Sometimes my upset sounds mad. But I'm glad she's okay."

"Yeah, but we're not so sure that she *is* okay. Something's wrong. All of us feel it. We just don't know what."

He sighed. Maybe weary of all of us and our vibes.

I decided to go for it. What the hell, it had been a rough day. "You know," I said to him, conversationally. Evenly. But maybe not in my sweet voice. "You've always been cold to me. And hard. You can't be like that to Asia. It made me so miserable, for as long as I can remember." *Take that, ice-man.*

He took his time, sipping his coffee. "Oh, I can't take all the credit, Dylan. You were miserable long before you met me."

I sucked in some hot coffee and tried to deny it.

He continued. "Men = problems. Isn't that how'd you say it?"

How would he know what I'd say? "But," I argued, "when Grey was born, you changed. You got even colder. At least to me."

Silence flitted into the room while we looked at each other over our coffee. We drank and stared. Silence pulled up a chair.

"No, I think not," he said after a while. "When Grey was born, you pulled away. Like somehow I'd betrayed you."

I put my cup down. "I did not."

He nodded and pursed his lips. "Did, too," he said wryly. Or maybe that was him looking sad. "And now Asia is, too."

"Well, don't freeze her out. You've got to drown her in love."

"Dylan, I didn't freeze you out. You were mad I had a son."

"That can't be right. I love Grey. I always have."

"I didn't say you were mad at Grey."

No, that absolutely could not be right. Grant was nothing to me. Leila had done what she'd said she'd do, found someone different, an exact opposite of Drew. I'd never wanted Grant or his love. Or anything to do with him.

"And anyway," his voice got lower, "that's what your mother does. Drowns you and Asia. Trying to make up for something. It throws everything out of balance. Nothing I do is good enough."

"Well, you're a stepparent. You have to try harder."

"What? Act differently with you than I do with Grey?"

"I wouldn't worry about that," I said. "No stepparent ever treated their step-kids the same as their own. They turn away, facing their own blood-child. They don't even see the steps." I paused a minute and thought about that. I liked it; the image was just right. "Listen. I'm an expert on this stuff."

He shrugged, unswayed by my expertise. "Maybe. But I think step-kids purposely stand behind you. Out of your reach. So how can you make everyone feel loved? Your own kids as well as the angry little ones you inherit? I just know how to be fair."

"Where's Mama?" Grey said, lurching into the room, rubbing his eyes and climbing up into my lap.

I kissed his hair. "She's fine, just catching her breath."

"Because of Asia," he nodded sagely.

"Yeah," I said. Grant didn't say a word. He was the outsider now, sitting there watching us. Wasn't that the essence of a stepfamily? Somebody was always going to be left out?

"I know what's wrong," Grey said. "What I've been feeling."

"What?" I asked, the way you ask little kids when they say they know something. Not as though you're expecting any big news.

"Asia's dad got dead."

Suddenly, I knew it was true. Drew was dead. *Oh, my poor little Asia. Looking for something that's already gone.*

"I'm right, aren't I?" he asked. I nodded my cheek on his head. "And you know what? It makes me sad for Asia. Everybody needs a daddy," he said, looking across at his. He left my lap to go climb up in Grant's, facing me. Grant wrapped his arms around him and once he got comfortable,

Grey announced, "You'd have picked up on it, too, except you're too stressed out."

"Let's go tell your mom," Grant said in Grey's ear, looking up at me from under his brow. "She'll want to know about this."

And so that's what we did, piling into his big Mercedes and driving the few blocks to Leila's motel. We didn't have to tell her. She already knew.

"Our poor little Asia," she cried, reaching up to stroke Grant's face with the back of her finger. He gave her a look. "Freaking out is just my way of coping, you know."

"Since when?" he asked.

"Since always before," she said after a beat.

"I liked it better the other way, our way," he said softly.

She nodded at him and smiled.

"Can we go home now?" he said, and I knew he was about to add something like "Some of us have to work" but he didn't.

We walked out of the cold motel room, shut the door and left. Leila traveled light. But, then, she always had.

When we got back, Leila walked Grey up to his bedroom. I could hear worried voices all the way up the stairs.

That's when Grandma Frank called.

"You know," was her greeting.

"About Drew?" I asked, just to be safe. You never knew what Grandma Frank might know that you didn't. Her silence confirmed it. "Yeah. We know," I said. "Grey had to tell us."

She chuckled, proud of her tuned-in descendant.

"I couldn't call before," she said. "Asia and I needed to talk first. And we have been, for hours."

"How is she?" I asked, and knew it was a dumb question. She'd been waiting her whole life to find her daddy.

"It's not a dumb question, Sky, darling," Grandma Frank said. "You love her. She's upset but she's going to be okay."

"Can I talk to her?"

"She's asleep. We'll be there tomorrow. You can talk then."

"Give her my love."

"Send it yourself. We've both been feeling it all day."

The thought sent a warm buzz through my body.

"Grandma Frank?" I needed to know something else.

Except, I didn't need to ask. "A man by the restrooms asked her for directions. While he was stoking his wonker."

"What?" Did my grandma just say, "stoking his wonker"?

"I did," she said. "Asia grabbed onto the staircase railing and started shrieking at the top of her strong little lungs. The guy almost fainted but he got away. Wonker flapping. The ticket agents kept Asia close until I could get there and receive my lecture on a bus station being no place for little girls."

A chunk of dread floated off my shoulder. "How did Drew...?"

"Overdose," she said. "Accidental. Not long after he left."

So that's why he was the only one to truly let Leila go. "Wow, Grandma Frank, you always know everything."

"Psychic. Plus I've got a friend at the sheriff's office."

When I got off the phone, I filled Grant in on the latest.

"She okay?" A concerned father this time, not a mad one.

I nodded with my ironic smile. For the new him. The new us.

"I always thought you wanted me to leave you alone. Thought you wanted to have just one father. I'm sorry." The warmth I felt might have been a thaw in the Step Freeze. He smiled at me.

"Yeah," I said, "I can see that." And it just shows how rotten I was that his smile still looked to me like the big bad wolf's. Grandma, what big teeth you have!

20

I WOKE WITH A SMILE, my skin at rest. A rare occurrence at Step Away's—I mean, Grant's—house. The smile was usually crawling off as soon as I opened my eyes and realized where I was. But not this glorious morning. Life was good. And all things were possible. Even Brad. Especially Brad. I could see that now.

It was Friday and the family, minus my poor little Asia, left for school and work. And I—conscientious employee that I was—made several truly inspired sales calls. After each one, I sloughed off the snubs and condescending attitudes reserved exclusively for salespeople, took a deep breath and checked for messages. Because I'd awakened knowing I couldn't give up on Brad. He was The One and I was going to have to trust him to find time in his crazy life for me. Anything was possible.

Rational disagreed. *Brad will always be gone*, she sneered. *Even if he was here.*

I didn't listen. Rational was lousy at love.

While I waited for his call, the new me, the optimistic me, had a busy day ahead. First, there was the wedding rehearsal to get through, the dry run for number twelve, Wedding of the Millennium. New Me had a little trouble with her newfound enthusiasm. But I dragged myself over to the church with the bounce of Marie Antoinette to the guillotine and, wonder of wonders, most glorious of days, it went pretty well. Except for the part about having a groom on crutches.

And while I waited for Dr. Sphincter to hobble down the aisle, I checked for messages. Twenty-two times. No Brad. Yet.

The dinner was next and no International Summit had been given more thought or planning. Everything was going to be perfect. It had to be. I'd even printed out an info sheet from the Internet to focus my planning, to flood me with inspiration. *Tips For the All-Important Rehearsal Dinner.*

When the evening was over, I made my own notes on the tip sheet. For future reference.

Tip 1: The guest list for the rehearsal dinner includes the wedding party, parents, immediate family and officiating church members. Spouses and dates should also be invited. Many couples include out-of-town guests.

We'd decided against packing all the disparate groups into a single dinner. We'd segregated Ron's one-up Dallas cronies at the ill-fated Provençal luncheon and Eva's out-of-town relatives at Le Bistro. So this dinner would be just for our Austin friends. Even the groomsmen were all Eva's buddies. Apparently Dr. Sphincter didn't have anyone close enough. Wonder why.

A lot of these friends used to date each other in school. But the Diamond Girls had developed a fondness for older men, tanned and polished and prosperous enough to give them what they needed most. Our guy friends still hung out with each other, having fun, trying to keep the party going.

Note to self: While it had seemed like a good idea at the time, it wasn't.

Tip 2: A cocktail party may be held before the dinner. However, it should be short, as excessive drinking can spoil the evening.

We arrived at the hotel for the dinner more than an hour late. It had taken a lot longer to rehearse with the walking wounded than we'd thought. But Terrell was there, playing host, urging everyone to frequent the open bar. No one seemed the least concerned about punctuality issues. In fact, they were all downright jolly, especially the ex-frat boys. I thought they were a little loud. I checked for messages.

Note to self: The cocktail party should be no more than ten minutes. *Max.*

Tip 3: The rehearsal dinner should have a different style and menu than the wedding. If the wedding is a formal sit-down dinner, then the rehearsal dinner should be more casual. And never serve the same type of meal at both.

Eva wanted French food. At everything. Probably even for breakfast. And in Eva-world, casual was a four-letter word. So formal and French it was. And to Eva that meant escargot.

We'd just gotten seated at the beautifully set U-shaped table when the platters of the greasy little slimers began to arrive. Hundreds of them. Eva plucked one perfect little brown shell from the oil as soon as the dish was set in front of her.

Sean, Ron's twin and best man, sat next to her, looking quite dashing. He'd brought a hottie, just like Ron had said he would. A young, bouncy blonde with big teeth and Dallas red lipstick. It was plain why things hadn't worked out between Sean and me. Even the New Me couldn't pull off that kind of exuberance.

As the escargot was being served, this lovely young girl with the West Texas twang felt the urge to share with her table neighbor—me!—her own extraordinary experience with snails.

"I used to be able to eat escargot when I was little. My daddy thought it made a good impression to eat that sort of thing," she said confidentially. But voices like hers aren't made for secrets and everyone just sat there, forks poised for the thrust, and listened in. "But then one summer our gardener had this *awful* problem with slugs in the flower beds, just eatin' up everything in sight. He put out little saucers of beer so they'd fall in 'em and drown."

I looked around for some other conversation to join. There were none.

"Well, the next weekend, we were eating breakfast out on the patio, when the wind shifted and that horrible, rotting-dead-animal smell—you know? You never, ever mistake it for anything else—hit us right in the face. My mama started gagging and ran into the house, all hunched over in her silk bathrobe. My daddy and I stuck our napkins over our noses and walked down the path to the flower beds by the pool house. We followed that stink like a trail."

Poor Sean, apropos of nothing, said, "Meagan's family is in oil, over in Odessa. They're close friends with the Bushes."

She looked at him for a second, and then came back to me, her words all slurred and breathy. "They must've come from miles away," she drawled. "Millions of 'em. Snails with shells. Slugs without 'em. And they were all deader than dead. Stinkin'. On top of each other. Oozin' and rottin' in that hot summer sun."

Nobody said a word as she paused for a sip of wine. Not even Sean. We all just sat there, our little forks in the air.

"My daddy was so mad he went and fetched the gardener. He told Daddy he hadn't plucked out the dead ones because it worked best that way. And it kept on getting better and better. You see," she said and looked around, talking to the whole table now, "what first gets them is the beer, then it's that stink. That's what they come for—those decom-posin' bodies."

Silence gagged.

No one ate.

Some of the friskier guys thought it would be fun to fling snails at each other. Maybe we shouldn't have had them altogether like this.

Note to self: No garden pests on the menu. Even French ones.

Tip 4: You should consider serving the groom's cake. Some brides are getting creative, making it in various shapes to match the groom's personality.

Dinner was almost done and I felt quite fuzzy. Everyone looked a little fuzzy, too. There hadn't been much eating going on, not after the snail's tale. But we'd all consumed our share of the excellent French wine. Okay, really, three times our share. It was one of those nights, the kind that called for sedation. My eyes wandered up and down the length of the table. Not a designated driver in sight.

The uneaten food was cleared away, our wineglasses refreshed. It was time. I gave a signal to the head waiter and the lights dimmed and the pianist in the corner—who'd assured me he could find the keys in the dark—began singing the Beatles' song that Eva had picked out for Ron. "Can't Buy Me Love."

What did I know, maybe she really did love the guy. Maybe she'd love him even if he was poor, starting a new company, with a ratty old car and an empty apartment.

Could Ron really be Eva's soul mate?

Nah, Rational scoffed. *It's the diamonds.*

I had some more wine and wondered where the groom's cake was. I'd nixed the idea of creating a cake to match Dr. Sphincter's personality—too gross. So, the plan was for a three-layer chocolate masterpiece to be secretly rolled out on a cart in the dark by a waiter dressed all in black. Everyone's attention would be on the guy singing, no one would notice. When the cake reached Ron's side, the waiter was to light it. One match, and three layers of sparklers would explode into life.

I was thinking about Brad when I had one of my epiphanies. A midsong one. *Eva is going to spend her whole life with a man she doesn't love. Just for some diamonds.* The thought made me sad—or maybe it was the wine.

The song was going to be over and the cake still hadn't arrived. I was tired and a little sick but I knew I had to get up and check. Something had to go right for once. For Eva. I jumped to my feet, like I imagined I'd do if I was sober, and crashed into the cart coming the wrong way.

The pianist banged to a stop and the lights came on. I couldn't move. The cake and I were one. Double dark chocolate fudge iced my naked back. Along with several sparklers. Think porcupine.

I stood there, marshalling dignity, while the waiters attempted to defrost me. The room had exploded into hysterics. My ex-buddies screamed. One fell out of his chair. Two others came over to lick my back. And then I knew. Brad was never going to call. He was too damn busy. And if he cared at all, he didn't care enough. I stood there, blinking away tears.

Note to self: Keep the lights on.

21

ASIA AND Grandma Frank heard me in the kitchen, scarfing down a banana, searching for vitamins and Advil. Preparing for the worst hangover of my life. Asia ran into my arms and we hugged for hours. Grandma Frank joined in and the three of us stood there by the jagged-edge granite island, arms wrapped tight, charging our auras. Grandma Frank pulled away to make us a pot of herbal tea—something for my stomach and head, she said—while Asia and I continued our commune. When the tea was ready, we all sat down at the breakfast table with our steaming mugs and had a sip of the mysterious brew. "Tell me," I said.

"Your back's kind of sticky," Asia said, feeling her hand.

"Don't change the subject!"

"It's chocolate!" She sniffed. "What happened to *you*?"

"I don't want to talk about it," I grunted. The evening had been unsalvageable after my run-in with the cake. Really from the get-go. We'd gone ahead and lit the sparklers, against our better judgment. It had taken about twenty matches to get them all going and the whole time we were messing with it our ex-friends were oohing and aahing like it was the Fourth of July. We'd heard serious proposals for a food fight.

Eva, Ron and their families left without cutting the cake. The Diamond Girls and their older dates followed close behind. I watched these guys with new admiration. It had occurred to my wine-thickened brain sometime during the

Animal House evening that these gentlemen were supplying something more precious than diamonds to their young female companions. Dignity, maturity, class. Nonexistent in the guys our age, the whole infantile lot of them. Men. I liked the sound of it. The thought made me look closer at these guys, made me notice that they were in better shape than our juvenile friends. Better-looking, better dressed. Lots more style. Especially Sean, so tall and elegant. Too bad I wasn't blond. And rich. Loud. Brainless...

"Come on, Asia," I said, pushing thoughts of Snail Girl away. "Tell me about your adventure." She looked so young, sitting there in her jeans and yellow T-shirt. Her hair was pulled back in some kind of fancy braid. Grandma Frank's weaving handiwork, no doubt.

"About what?"

"About how brave you were. Hanging on and screaming like you did," I told her. "That was awesome."

"I saw it on TV," she said, shrugging, as though it was no big deal, as though she thwarted bad guys every day before lunch.

"Are you okay?" I asked.

"Not yet," she answered, her face scrunching up, trying hard not to cry. I held my free arm out to her and she crawled up in my lap like Grey always did, like she used to before she got cool. We sat there a long time, me holding Asia and Grandma Frank holding my hand. And I talked to Asia about her daddy, told her stuff I hadn't thought to tell her before. About the paintings he made of the desert, the ones with the lightning that looked so real you'd swear you were staring at a storm out your window. And how he didn't own a pair of pants that weren't jeans and he didn't own a pair of jeans that didn't have paint on them. And how that was okay because in New Mexico they liked artists more than anybody else. And how Drew's work was better than good. It was magic. And then I had to stop my own tears.

"Why did he leave me?" she asked a fingernail. The one she'd been studying the whole time I'd been talking.

This was too hard. "He didn't leave you, little one," I said and laid my head against hers. I took a breath and went on. "He never even saw you. He couldn't have left if he had, that's why he took off in such a hurry. Scared. He was running because he didn't have a father himself. Didn't think he'd ever be good enough."

"Was he?"

I thought about him waiting for me every day after the bus, with his hands in his pockets, that solemn look on his face. And then I heard him behind the bedroom door, screaming at Leila, panicked at the very thought of a baby. "I don't know," I told her. "I honestly don't know."

She didn't speak for a few minutes, thinking sad thoughts. And then she asked what she'd been wondering all along, ever since she'd found he was gone. "Do you think he'd have tried to find me, later, I mean, if he'd lived and all?"

"I'm sure of it," I told her. "Aren't you? Almost everybody grows up eventually." I grinned at Grandma Frank and leaned down to whisper in Asia's ear. "Even Grant."

"Grant's my daddy," she sighed. "All the daddy I got now."

"Yeah," I said. "Looks like." I let it hang in the air awhile before I added, "Maybe he could be my daddy, too." She twisted around to look me in the face. Apparently I hadn't hidden my views on the man as well as I thought. "Well," I argued with her skeptical look. "My real one's kind of busy and we could do worse, you and I."

"Whoa," she said. "How much did you drink tonight?"

"Nunya," I huffed. Then I rolled one eye up into my head and let the other eyelid flutter down. "A lot."

She nodded as she got out of my lap. "That's what I thought." She stood behind Grandma Frank, wrapped her arms around the bony shoulders and kissed a wrinkly cheek. She was going to be okay. We both were.

"So do you have any thoughts on my love life, Grandma?" I asked, feeling lighter by the minute. That was some good tea. "I could sure use some good news."

"You give me too much credit, Sky," she said as she stood up and stretched. "I don't know who or when, I just know that he'll find you. When it's time."

It wasn't nearly as late as it could have been if the rehearsal dinner had gone well and we'd celebrated long into the night. Grandma Frank made her way to the downstairs guest wing and Asia and I went upstairs to my bedroom. She dove in under my covers and we talked ourselves hoarse about weddings. What did I think about Eva's wedding plans? Toppo, absolutely Toppo. And what did I want mine to be like? Can I get back to you later on that?

"Well, you better hurry," she said. "All your friends are already getting married."

Yeah, thanks for pointing that out.

When we couldn't focus our eyes any longer and our mouths started hanging open even after we'd stopped speaking, Asia climbed out of my bed and headed for her own. Note to self: quit being so snotty about the seven bedrooms. They're damned convenient. I stretched out, luxuriating in the space, and promptly passed out. Or maybe the wine had nothing to do with it and I just didn't want to have to think anymore.

"I LOVE HAVING YOU HOME!" Leila cried as she jumped onto my bed early the next morning and got in under the covers with me. I could feel her wiggling around getting comfortable, piling up the pillows just right. "Let's go into business together," she said, leaning over and dropping her voice to a whisper in my still-snoozing ear. "We can start a consulting firm. I'm selling Fantasy Faux and that'll give us enough money to get it set up right. We won't have to bother with outside financing."

I put my arm over my face.

"We'll specialize in collaborative browsing. Oh, I love the sound of it. Hear those words. *Feel* that karma," she said switching to her normal voice, soft and sexy, not so very different from the whispering. If she hadn't already made a huge success of one business—a business carrying exactly zero debt load—you might think she'd done a bit too much mind expansion back in the day. Like to the breaking point.

But no one should be that enthusiastic—about anything—before, say, ten in the morning. "You'll be the president, of course. That's only fair since you have the current expertise. And we won't do any of the coding or the integration ourselves. We'll be gate keepers. Design the plan, own it, make sure everything gets implemented exactly according to our vision specs. That's what we'll call them. You like it? Vision Specs."

No. Not at seven in the morning. I put a pillow on my face. Silence joined me and tried to go back to sleep.

"What do you think?" I heard her say through the feathers.

"I'll let you know when I'm out of therapy," I mumbled.

"I brought you coffee."

Well, why didn't she say so? It'd be all cold and awful now. I took the pillow off my face and looked over at the bedside table. There was my favorite mug, with the hand-painted sunflowers, a saucer balanced on top, keeping it toasty. I struggled to sit halfway up, stole one of the pillows from Leila's stack and reached for the mug. Coffee in bed = heaven.

"I love you," I said, and took a giant sip.

She kissed the top of my head. "Think about it," she whispered, as she slid down from the bed. "Think about it hard."

So I lay there on the high, soft bed, drinking my coffee, staring up at the faux-painted ceiling, thinking about Brad. Except the thoughts weren't really about him—I was just wondering how I could ever replace him.

Grey came screeching into the room and jumped on top of me just as I set the empty cup on the table.

"Grey! It's a sign. Everything's going to be okay."

"That's good," he agreed, diving way down deep under my covers. Good thing I knew to wear some kind of pajamas when I stayed there. He popped back up to ask, "What is?"

"My luck has changed," I said. "You could have come in a few seconds before and my coffee would have spilled. It could have burned you. Or me. And we'd have been all puckered up and red for the wedding. But it didn't. Hooray!" Amazing, the difference caffeine made in my personality.

Grey grunted and snuggled back in.

"Where is everybody?" I asked the lump beside me.

"Mama and Daddy are downstairs and Asia and Grandma Frank are still asleep with strict orders for everyone not to wake them," he said, wiggling in farther.

"Everyone?"

There was a pause. "Mostly me," came the muffled reply.

Then he popped up out of the covers. "Eva's on the phone," he said, eyes wide. "I forgot to tell you. That's why I came."

"Grey!"

"Sorry. I forgot."

"Well, she's gone now," I told him. "Eva's never hung around on hold in her life."

"Call her back."

"I can't. I don't want to talk to her." Ron would blame me for last night's disaster. For all the disasters.

But what if she needs something? This was her wedding day, after all. I called.

"I'm sorry about last night," I said after she'd picked up on the first ring. An all-time first.

"Yeah, well..." she said, dismissing it. "I need a favor."

"I figured."

"We have to get a groomsman," she said. "To replace Craig."

"Why? What happened to Craig?" He was the one who fell out of his chair.

"He slid down the stairs in his apartment," Eva said. "I think he was drunk."

You think? "It's too late to get a replacement now, Eva."

"No, it's not. Matt can do it."

I needed a minute to consider what to say about that.

"You know, don't you." It wasn't even a question.

"Yeah. I do."

"What do you want me to say?" she asked, seven of the most infuriating words in the English language. Right up there with "you people."

"You don't have to say anything. It's your life."

"I can hear your displeasure."

"No, you can't. If you want Matt, it's none of my business. Maybe it's your conscience you're hearing."

She blew out a French-sounding puff of air. "You're probably right. But, I've been punished enough, don't you think? These last few days have been a nightmare."

I couldn't argue with that. "Are you still seeing him?"

"You know, this is your fault," she whispered. "I was trying so hard to be a virgin—God! How do you do it?—and he called me up, all depressed because you'd dumped him at the wedding."

"You're still in love with him."

"*Vraiment.* I know," she said. I'd expected her to deny it.

"Oh, Eva," I sighed. "What's going to happen? Are you just going to keep having affairs all your life?"

"No. It's not like that. It's just that I couldn't stand it. And I can only be with Matt just a little while longer. After I'm married, things will be different. He and I can be friends then." *Wish it and it will be true.*

"He's okay with that?" I asked, already knowing the answer.

"He has to be," she sighed.

What a mess. I didn't want to think about it anymore. "Eva, you need to start getting ready."

"Okay. Just call me up and suggest it."

"Suggest what?"

"That Matt be the groomsman."

"Why?"

"Because it can't be my idea. I want him to come and he wants to be there. He thinks it will give him closure. Like going to a funeral."

Matt and Eva were perfect together. He was as nutty as she.

"Eva, you're not making any sense. Why do *I* have to call? I think it's a *terrible* idea. It'd be better to have a lopsided number of attendants."

"Just do this for me, please. It's all going to work. I promise you."

And she was right. She told Ron about my plan when I called. And asked him if he thought it would be okay while I was still on the line. She made her voice soft and hesitant. Like, maybe *she* didn't think it was such a good idea. He wanted to know if I couldn't come up with anything better than that, but time was getting short and he finally agreed.

I just hoped she didn't deliver Craig's tuxedo to Matt that morning herself. She wasn't married yet.

22

GROOM DADDY was there. At the wedding. I swear.

Andie and I were waiting in the staging area of the church with the other bridesmaids. We'd opened the little door into the sanctuary a crack so we could watch the priest leading in the groom and his attendants. Ron was walking athletically, easily, no crutches, no hint of a limp. *What was he on?*

We were all in our fabulous dresses, blues and indigos and violets. Eva's theme was the End of the Rainbow—to spell it out for anyone who didn't know, Dr. Sphincter was a Pot of Gold. The bridesmaids had been allowed to choose any dress within the end-of-rainbow color range, the only stipulation being that it had to be floor-length and modest enough for the catholic ceremony. We looked like the jewels in Ali Baba's cave. Mine was a sleek, strapless, midnight blue number. With a slit up my thigh. I felt slim. I felt beautiful. And I felt *good*.

Andie was squeezing in next to me, trying to see out the crack, too. Her dress met none of Eva's criteria. Color, style or probity. The burgundy was closer to start-of-the-rainbow red and the bias-cut silk layers hovered about midcalf. But what got your attention, what had you slumping over with your head hanging off your neck was the neckline. Low-cut and spaghetti strapped doesn't quite describe it. It barely covered her nipples. Or maybe it didn't. Eva had almost passed out when Andie tried it on for her. I could hear Eva mentally kicking herself for allowing me to talk her out of the standard French blue cardboard-satin dresses she'd originally selected. But then Andie slipped on the hand-made lace bolero jacket and promised she'd keep it on. Eva was appeased. Andie was gorgeous.

And, anyway, Eva had had her own improper bosom display to worry about. Think bimbo boobs. I know, I should talk. We'd found her a sheer, silk chiffon body suit to wear under her gown and when pearls were sewn in drifts at the ends of the sleeves, it was perfect, like a part of the dress. Eva loved it. Mostly because the teardrop diamond solitaire necklace Ron gave her for the wedding looked better—bigger!—on the chiffon.

So there we were in the small room off the foyer, the bridesmaids, the little ring bearer and the flower girls, all in blues and violets—and burgundy—waiting with Eva for the Dallas Symphony orchestra to wallop out the bride's processional, our music cue. The crowd was enormous. All eight hundred or so of them. And that's when I saw him, Groom Daddy. Or at least the back of his fat, sweaty, neckless little head. I was trying to point him out to Andie. "See? Right there behind the lady in the big hat."

I walked down the aisle, my chin high, head straight, trying to catch sight of Groom Daddy again. I should have known he'd be coming. All the money in Texas was there. But thinking about Groom Daddy made me think of Brad, so I stopped looking. And blinked away the sting in my eyes.

The rest of the wedding was a blur, a breathtaking explosion of end-of-the-rainbow flowers and candles, baritone recitations and heavenly song from the angelic Texas Boys' Choir. I do remember the ring bearer stepping up to present the Swarovski crystal slipper Eva's father had had custom-made in Austria for her foot. With money he didn't have. But Eva had always loved Cinderella's story, especially the part about being carried off to his castle. The slipper was balanced on its velvet pillow, the ring nestled inside. Actually it was tied on, the ring bearer being four and all. Prisms of light danced around the church as he moved.

Ron and Eva looked into each other's eyes and whispered words of love, like uphold and understand, comfort and treasure. The awesome sound system in the church guaranteed that even the eight hundred and first person in the last pew could hear every intimate word. There wasn't a dry female eye in the place, including mine. How to be cynical in the face of such perfection?

The "I now pronounce you" part never came since they didn't say that in Catholic weddings and the rest of the service was a bit anticlimactic, but that was fine since we needed a moment to dry up and recover. And then the ceremony was over and music filled the church again. The littlest flower girl held Eva's train and the other two sprang out in front to scatter purple rose petals on the indigo carpet laid between the pews. I remembered to hand Eva back her bouquet and she and Ron floated down the aisle through the petals, making you think about wanting some of those drugs.

Sean held his hand out to me as we started down the aisle. We hadn't rehearsed it that way, but I smiled and gave him my hand. It was nice not walking out alone.

"Lovely," he whispered and I looked up at him, unsure what he meant. Oh. *Me!*

After maybe twelve hours of photographs, the valets—valets, you ask? For a Dallas wedding, of course!—brought out the white limos and we rode the short distance to the country club. It was a different place. But then the last time I'd seen it, it had the harried air of a war zone. Now it was Provence. Stacked stone arches, vine covered walls, purple-blue flowers.

"Zis way, mademoiselle." Our handsome young escorts with musical accents and wild French shoes waltzed us from the porte cochere to the ballroom. "Ze wezzer ees nice today, *oui*?"

I glided on the arm of my spice-scented escort through a corridor draped with jewel-tone brocade and filled with purple flowers in country baskets and knew Eva's dream had come true. I'd spent the past ten months thinking miserly thoughts, pooh-poohing the egregious waste of funds—and few people pooh-poohed as well as I. Only Asia, that I can think of. But if you've got it, why not? Why settle for ordinary when you can have paradise?

The party was well underway when we got there, hundreds of guests milling and mingling, drinking champagne. Swooning over caviar morsels and bits of *foie gras*. We'd cancelled the escargot. The band was playing Faith Hill's "This Kiss" and they sounded great. Finding a band agreeable to large cross sections of the population is not really difficult, it's impossible. And we'd needed two so that there'd be live music the whole time. People were listening and standing with their heads tilted to the side, swaying, just waiting for the newlyweds to dance the first dance. Whew! One less worry, another sigh of relief.

Eva had opted out of a reception line, declaring it middle-class and tacky, so she and Ron began working the room as soon as we arrived. But first she caught my hand and pulled me in for a hug.

"*Merci, merci, merci bien*," she cooed. "It's perfect." She kissed one of my cheeks and then the other and promptly forgot I was standing there.

I noticed—and I didn't have to be terribly observant—that she'd removed the body suit on the way over. Her gown—and her body—were perfection in the opulent setting of the ballroom, not a bit tacky. Just French.

I found two pieces of my family smack-dab in the center of things. Leila was deep in conversation with Eva's mom. Grey ran up and threw his arms around me, burying his face in my waist. *Please, don't have gotten into the crêpes yet, Grey. Or if you did, have wiped your mouth really well.* "You're the most beautiful thing in the whole world," he said, looking up at me, arms still tight. "Better than anybody!"

Wow. Who cared about a few grease stains? I kissed the top of his spiky brown head and listened in on the conversation.

"I notice you're not wearing blood on your hands," Mrs. Aguirre said, squinting her eyes at Leila.

Oh, God, no.

"That's right," Leila smiled. She wore a beautiful yellow dress, echoes of the India prints back in her day but updated, silky and clinging with a bright red halter strap tied around her neck. I looked at her hands, too. Her only jewelry, besides the simple platinum wedding band, was a wide silver bracelet with a dangling coin, a gift from a friend. With her hair piled up, she looked twenty-two. No, she didn't really. She didn't have enough makeup on for twenty-two. Her look was more timeless beauty, when age was beside the point. As if that could ever be.

"But it's not because I had any sense or knew anything about blood diamonds," she said. "I'm from New Mexico. We don't go in much for flaunting. Unless we're talking turquoise or silver, then there's no such thing as too much."

Mrs. Aguirre's face softened. You could tell she approved. "I want to tell you a little secret," she said, leaning in close and looking over her shoulders both ways, in a campy pantomime of getting ready to dish. "My daughter's diamond isn't perfect," she sniffed. Another look, this way and that. "Eva had to choose between a massive, seriously flawed diamond or a smaller, perfect one. A much smaller one." Pause for effect. "She chose defective." She spat out the words. "For appearances." She lifted her head then, eyes zigzagging around the sumptuous room and said to herself, "I live in a place where nothing is real."

I half expected Leila to share her take on the subject and say something like "Real is what you want it to be." But just then Grant came up with two flutes of champagne.

"What's for appearances?" he asked affably, handing Leila her glass and offering the other one to Mrs. Aguirre, who rallied herself and took it from him. Eagerly.

Leila leaned into Mrs. Aguirre, exactly imitating the woman's earlier stance. "I don't think we should share this with anyone, do you?" she asked kindly, doing the shoulder peek. "You wouldn't want it to get out and reflect badly on your family." She turned to Grant and took his arm. "Let's get you something to drink," she said and dragged him away to anyplace but there.

Mrs. Aguirre wrinkled her forehead, staring at the ground. Then she tossed down the champagne and handed me the glass. Just like I'd done to Matt at number eleven. *How rude!* I needed to apologize for that. But now I needed to escape, too, to anyplace but there. I dumped the glass on a passing tray and went to look for Asia and Grandma Frank and found them listening to the band just as the lead guitar released the haunting notes for Eva's song.

Grandma Frank flipped her violet handwoven shawl over one shoulder, put her arm around my waist and said evenly, conversationally, as though she made pronouncements like it everyday, which she did, "He's close, my love. I can feel him."

Here? Now? I looked around the room.

"Are you sure?" Her look told me I needed to quit asking her that.

I think I already knew it. That he was there, that it was my day, too. A stillness flowed through my body with the haunting French song and I waited for him to come find me.

Ron led his bride onto the dance floor. Who knew? Who even suspected? The man could dance. Man, could the man dance. Where was the wounded wonk on crutches? This guy was tall and slim and strong and skimmed Eva around the floor as if they were on wheels. The wide skirt of her gown—with the train tucked up into a bustle—floated to one side then swayed back to the other. They danced like they do in black-and-white movies. Like a dream.

"Oh," Andie said as she came up behind me. "I get it now." She'd kept her promise, the lace jacket was still on. Warm brown skin was peering through the holes in the lace. Lots and lots of it. Making it sexier with the peek-a-boo jacket on than if she'd just taken it off. Andie, I'm sure, already knew that.

I grinned as we watched them, my eyes never leaving their dance. "This sets the bar kind of high, doesn't it?" I asked. "How could you be happy with an ordinary wedding after this?"

"Who says I would have been?" she huffed.

Maybe she was right. Maybe this was what everyone wanted. To create your own cloud nine and then dance on top of it. I wondered if I'd ever get the chance to decide. I looked around. *Where is he? Who is he?* The band slid into "Lady in Red."

"They gonna play every hokey song ever made?" Andie asked.

"Yeah, that's the plan," I answered, leaning my head a bit to the side and swaying. "Tell me about Terrell."

"What about him?"

"Do you think he's The One?"

"Damn, ain't he pretty! But he's only a high school coach."

I never knew if she was just trying to get a reaction.

Terrell came up beside Andie then and slipped his huge hand into hers and led her out to dance. He stood there a minute, holding her at arm's length, burning her up with his eyes, as if such a magnificent creature couldn't really exist. Then he pulled her in and swallowed her up, wrapping himself around her, looking not so much like he was dancing as protecting her. They swayed together, not quite moving their feet. They were beautiful. Shivers went up my arms.

Whoever he was, he needed to come find me. Now.

I floated up to the band to make my announcement. About it being time for everyone to find their names on the place cards and sit. To eat. Some more. And then I drifted down again.

Matt caught my hand as I wafted passed him. "Dyl," he said. "I just wanted to say...Dyl, you look incredible..."

Matt? Is it Matt?

"*Bonjour*, Matt. *Merci*," I cooed and tiptoed to kiss him on one cheek and then the other. Eva was right. The French knew how to do this stuff right. "You look quite dashing yourself."

"Who'd you come with?" he asked, still holding my hand.

"I don't know yet," I said, before I drifted away to my table. I didn't look back to see what he thought.

The next puff of time was a perfect blend of heavenly food and the best wine I'd ever tasted—and I'd been doing my share of that lately. A perfect meal spiced with flattering toasts. People were dancing in between courses, during some of them. That's how Eva had wanted it. A seamless movement from drink to food to dance and back. I swayed in my chair. *Where is he?*

"Are you okay?" Asia asked me about every three minutes.

I didn't answer.

"I think she's melting, Grandma Frank," Asia said. "Help her or there's going to be one hell of a mess on her chair."

Leila turned from her conversation with the cardiac surgeon on her right to beam Asia her "young lady!" look.

Asia knew enough to try to look chastised and gave Grant a little shrug. He shook his head at her, smiling.

"She's fine," said Grandma Frank. "She's just happy."

"Are you sure?" Asia asked. "She's acting dopey like Eva."

"Yes, I'm sure," huffed Grandma Frank. Then she grinned at me.

"Which one of my girls would like to dance?" Grant asked.

Leila moved her head a quarter-turn toward him and smiled but kept on with her conversation. Something about polluted lakes in Russia.

"Why, I'd be delighted," Asia said, rising from her seat. She'd worn a skirt for the occasion. And her T-shirt was long sleeved with sequined paisleys. Downright black-tie for Asia.

"I have a surprise for you," he told her.

Asia looked at him, waiting.

Her cynical look in place.

"I've located one of your father's paintings," he said coming around the table to her, offering his arm. "They're shipping it out to you from New Mexico next week."

Leila stopped her conversation to watch Asia, who just stood there, paralyzed, eyes wide. Then she let out a whoop and whirled into him, ignoring his offered arm, and pressed her face to his chest, wrapping her thin arms all the way around him and hugging him tight. Grant pulled a crisp, white handkerchief from his coat pocket, leaned back a bit to dab her face and silently led her out to the dance floor. They had a little trouble in the beginning, some confusion about whose arms went where, and then they were dancing. Straight-legged and boxy. Asia grinned as though her teeth were too big for her mouth and Grant looked about as pleased as a finance guy could. Grandma Frank, Leila and I all got sappy grins on our faces, too.

"Will you dance with me?" Grey asked.

"Why, I'd be delighted," I replied. We made Asia and Grant look positively graceful. A few more minutes of it and neither of us would ever dance again.

"May I?" Sean came up and tapped Grey on the shoulder.

"What's that supposed to mean?" Grey asked, turning to look at Sean over the tapped shoulder.

"I'd like to dance with your sister. May I cut in?"

Grey flopped his head back. "Is this the way it works?" he asked me.

I nodded and he dropped his arms and walked back to the table, the model of chivalry, except he kept muttering to himself, "Well, that's stupid."

Sean danced like his brother. As though we were on a cloud.

"I hope that was all right," he said, after a few twirls, after our bodies had become acquainted.

I smiled back at him, leaning into the spin.

We floated on air, as if we'd been dancing together for years. And every thought I had for the next several minutes was filtered through that fact. How well we moved together.

Where's Slug Girl? "I didn't see your date," I said, "the pretty blond girl from last night."

"We had what you'd call a tiff."

"Nope. I'm pretty sure I'd never say tiff."

He smiled and we didn't say anything else for a few bars.

"Let me guess," I said. "An argument started when you objected to the timing of her snail story. You said something like, 'What the *beep* were you thinking!'"

He grinned a little. Maybe at my authentic sounding censor-beep. I'd learned it from Asia's CDs, the ones edited for obscenity. There were so many beep-outs, they just incorporated them into the song.

"And you'd be right," he nodded, the grin growing.

Silence answered, letting me enjoy the dance. And then the next one. And the one after that. I could have danced forever.

Sean was tall and buff like his brother. I could feel the strength in his arm where it held my back. I wondered why he'd never asked me out again, after the first couple of times. Maybe I'd been sending the wrong message. Maybe I wasn't ready back then.

Is it Sean?

My thoughts whirled round the room. Sean was in property development; he was probably as rich as his brother. Maybe more so, with no malpractice to worry about. So what if this was my life? What if this was real? Would it be wonderful to be taken care of? To be a princess like Eva? To not have to work anymore and still have everything you wanted. What would that feel like? *Like this.* Floating.

Except you don't like to shop, Rational butted in. *You'd be bored stupid.*

Groom Daddy tapped Sean's shoulder.

My luck. Just when I think I'm a princess, I get waylaid by the ogre. Sean stepped aside, murmuring, "Forgive me, Doug. Of course. I've been hogging this beauty." A rodeo scene popped up in my head. Ropin' calves and hoggin' beauties.

What? Did all the rich guys in Texas know each other? And were they all really there in that room?

I gritted my teeth at monster man. "I think I'll take a little break." And started walking back to the table.

"Honey, you don't wanna do that." He grabbed me, jerking me back. I slammed into him and my ankle twisted off my heel.

Sean was standing a few feet off to the side, diplomatically observing the events as they unfolded. Such deference! Just how much money did Groom Daddy have?

"No, thank you," I said and calmly yanked my hand away.

Don't cause a scene, Rational cautioned.

Easy for her to say. She didn't have to worry about Groom Daddy sweat. Or his breath. Or his hands.

He caught my hand again and wrapped his ogre arm around my waist. I remembered how strong he was. The centaur. "Come on, darlin'." He squashed me into his chest. "We never got to finish that dance."

I couldn't believe it. What kind of miserable karma had I accumulated in my short lifetime to deserve this man? Twice! I looked at Sean to see how likely it was that he'd step with some assistance. It wasn't that I needed rescuing or anything. But he might have been able to pull it off with a little less noise.

But he was clearly deferring to Groom Daddy, not about to upset the man. Or his influence.

Well, I didn't need his money and I wasn't going to be dragged around by anybody. Ever again. I started rehearsing what I would do in my head. I'd try talking first. With just the right sound, the right mix of power, threat and appeal to reason. And if that didn't work, I'd follow Asia's example: Hang on and scream like hell.

"Ah, there you are!" someone said behind me. "Finally! I've been looking all over for you!"

Groom Daddy gave a little snort. I felt it against my belly. And I can't talk about that any more or I'll barf. Brad walked over to us and didn't look like he was going to stop until he went right over the top of Groom Daddy. The ogre half pushed me away and I staggered back in my heels.

Brad caught me around the waist, nodding to Groom Daddy. He was wearing his dark wedding suit and cowboy boots. And he looked better than anything I'd seen in my life. He pulled me to him and kissed my cheek and the couple bubble drifted down to protect us. Eight hundred people disappeared. Including the two rich guys. Poof. They were gone.

I turned my face to his hand on my shoulder and kissed the back of it.

His amazing mouth grinned and then he gave an ironic glance down at the floor and brushed his other hand against my cheek. "Sorry 'bout the boots," he said. "They lost my bags."

"They're wonderful," I said, turning to kiss that hand, too. I was so happy to see him, I would have kissed his boots if I didn't think it'd scare him. "You came!"

"Well, I had another damn epiphany, Sky."

"I like epiphanies," I said. "I have them often myself."

"Wanna hear it?"

I gave him a slow little nod, watching his eyes.

"Okay. I have to have you in my life. Whatever that takes."

I just kept nodding. And smiling. "Whatever?" I asked.

"Yeah," he said, wrapping both arms around me. "Anything."

"But what about your meeting?" I remembered to ask,

thinking it wouldn't be good if I messed things up for him at work. Not long-term. "You didn't miss it, did you?"

"No. I got my meeting done. I just didn't hang around for all the bullshit afterward."

"And…"

The grin returned. "We got the contract."

It was impossible to look at those lips and those beautiful teeth and not smile yourself. But, then again, I wasn't trying.

"Sky, we're going to need some heavyweight help with the collaborative browsing piece," he said, trying to get serious but not being able to do anything about the lopsided grin. "It's a big part of the deal. Matter of fact, we probably got the contract because I'd done so much research on it. Because I'd wanted to know what you did. See? It was fate, meeting you."

Whoa, fate. The word sent shivers to my flower child toes. "Glad I could help," I said, smiling, thinking, *research collaborative browsing? Because of me? That's got to be love!*

Sometime during all that conversation, we'd started to dance. Not whirling and dipping, just moving to the music, with our hands around each other's waists. Talking. Because we had a lot of catching up to do.

"So tell me how I do that. Contract with eBoost for your time now that you're in sales," he said.

"You don't. My mom and I are starting our own consulting firm. Vision Specs. You contract with me for my time." *That* had a nice ring.

"Since when?" he asked, surprised. And pleased.

"Since we knew it was the only way," I said, thinking that maybe this morning it sounded a little flighty. But it *was* the right decision. Even Rational thought so. And that was the kind of thing she was good at.

"Great. We can talk about the details later. But right now I'm more interested in some alone time than consulting time." He looked around the room for a minute, as though he was searching for a quiet place for us to hide. "This is really something," he said taking it all in.

"Do you like it?" Why did I ask questions I already knew the answer to? Just so my stomach could cramp up when I heard the response? How sick was that?

He looked away from the room, back into my eyes. "Yeah, it's nice, you know, if you like this sort of thing."

"But do *you* like it." Apparently, the twinge I felt wasn't enough of a cramp.

He smiled and pulled me closer to him. "You *know* it's not my kind of thing." Okay, now it was a cramp.

"Yeah? Well what is?"

He started dancing for real, whirling me around, his boots barely brushing the floor. He held my waist and watched my face.

You," he said, "are my kind of thing."

Even I knew enough to shut up after that.

A few more twirls, and he asked, "When will the princess be ready to leave this ball?"

I wanted to say, now, "Right now." Ah, the burden of conscientiousness. "I'm going to do a toast here in a minute. Then anytime…"

He tried to look okay with that but he wanted out of there. Badly. I could tell. I needed to let him go.

"Why don't I just meet you at your place?" I asked and looked him right in the eye when I said it.

"That would be fine," he said, looking back. "I'll be waiting." We'd stopped dancing. I don't know when. We were just standing there with our arms around each other's waists, gazing. He leaned down and kissed me. If we were an obstacle to other dancers you couldn't tell by me.

I watched him go then, walking tall and easy in his boots.

He stopped a few feet away and turned around to ask, "How's Guinness?"

"He's staying with friends and they tell me he's lonesome," I said. "That he misses me dreadfully."

"I missed you, too," he said. "Dreadfully?" he asked himself, and then nodded. "Yeah, dreadfully. And, you know what? My kind of thing is the girl that I love and me, a bunch of our friends, and some of our family, maybe even a big brown dog, and whatever else she wants that will make her happy."

Epilogue

I DROVE UP to his Spartan little apartment on the north edge of town. Everything was just as I remembered it. Exactly. Except the shoes were gone and there was a rock holding down one of the corners of the blueprint.

He met me at the door, smelling fresh, wearing a rumpled shirt and blue jeans. Sleeves rolled up. His feet were bare. I slipped off my high, strappy shoes and tiptoed to kiss him.

He pulled away and looked at my face, asking me the question with his eyebrows. Trying to avoid another freak-out?

I nodded my head just once. *Yes, my love. It's time.* He scooped me up without a word and carried me lightly in his arms down the hall to his room, nuzzling my neck, whispering, kissing my breasts above the midnight silk. I pondered the joys of hard, physical labor. Those muscles were not just aesthetic. Now I was truly floating. My feet off the floor, my head in the heavens, my heart in my throat. Brad shut the door to his room with his foot and locked Rational and Fear and that little girl who everyone left out in the hall. And we were alone.

I don't know what else was in the room. I saw only the bed, a feather-soft cloud, inviting. My clothes vanished, disappeared silky piece by silky piece, and he set me down naked on the cushion of air. I gazed at his eyes—well, not only his eyes—as he tore the clothes from his body, too. One bare knee leaned onto my cloud and he paused then, balanced on his hands, to return my gaze, to brush his dark eyes across my body. I could feel my body wanting to squirm, to wiggle out from under his stare, do anything to lessen that hunger in his face.

"Come with me, Sky," I heard in my head. "My beautiful Sky. Don't leave me."

His eyes locked onto mine as his chest, then his hips skimmed my legs and his lips reached down to kiss me. In all of those places girls need to be kissed.

"Come with me, Sky, come to me now."

Doors unfastened and barricades melted. That hard knot inside me turned from concrete to butter. And, one by one, the tight blue rubber bands popped off my heart.

All around us, walls disappeared. The roof opened up like a fist unfolding and the moon shone its light on our skin. His voice was in my head again and I heard his growly whisper. "I love you, Sky." I left his bed then and flew out into space, leaving my body behind, rocking to rhythms of passion. And just when I knew I couldn't be happier, when there was nothing in the world that could be better than this, I felt it, gripping like tension inside me. A glorious wave surging through me, heaving, tossing me, turning me, end over end. I was a star. Flaring, exploding, then bursting to life. When it ebbed, it left slowly. And that's when I smiled.

So did Brad as he lay on the pillow beside me. The tooth-iest, crookedest, happiest grin yet.

So did I get that right, was that what really happened? Or was his bedroom a place for a monk. With a hard narrow bed or maybe even a cot or a mat on the floor. And was it love or just dynamite sex? Sex way, way, way past due? What if that was all it was? Do it once every twenty-four years and you're gonna see stars!

So what *was* in my head and what was real? And how do you tell the difference?

No clue.

Who knew what small portion of reality I ever actually experienced? But I found I no longer cared. Like my mother said, real was what you wanted it to be, what made you happy.

And, right at that moment, in the caressing arms of the man I loved, I was very, very happy.

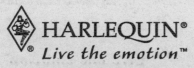

Harlequin Romance®

THE WEDDING PLANNERS

Where weddings are all in a day's work!

Have you ever wondered about the women behind the scenes, the ones who make those special days happen, the ones who help to create a memory built on love that lasts forever—who, no matter how expert they are at helping others, can't quite sort out their love lives for themselves?

Meet Tara, Skye and Riana—three sisters whose jobs consist of arranging the most perfect and romantic weddings imaginable—and read how they find themselves walking down the aisle with their very own Mr. Right…!

Don't miss the THE WEDDING PLANNERS trilogy by Australian author Darcy Maguire:

A Professional Engagement HR#3801

On sale June 2004 in Harlequin Romance®!

Plus:

The Best Man's Baby, HR#3805, on sale July 2004
A Convenient Groom, HR#3809, on sale August 2004

Available at your favorite retail outlet.

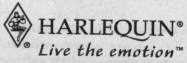

HARLEQUIN®
Live the emotion™

Visit us at www.eHarlequin.com

HRTWP

HARLEQUIN® *Blaze*™

HARLEQUIN® *Temptation*.

Single in South Beach

Nightlife on the Strip just got a little hotter!

Join author Joanne Rock as she takes you back to Miami Beach and its hottest singles' playground. Club Paradise has staked its claim in the decadent South Beach nightlife and the women in charge are determined to keep the sexy resort on top. So what will they do with the hot men who show up at the club?

GIRL GONE WILD
Harlequin Blaze #135
May 2004

DATE WITH A DIVA
Harlequin Blaze #139
June 2004

HER FINAL FLING
Harlequin Temptation #983
July 2004

Don't miss the continuation of this red-hot series from Joanne Rock!

Look for these books at your favorite retail outlet.

HBSSB2

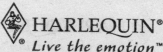

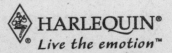